The

Diver

Alfred Neven DuMont

Translated by David Dollenmayer

The

Diver

St. Martin's Press  New York

The translation of this work was supported by a grant from the Goethe-Institut
GOETHE-INSTITUT, which is funded by the German Ministry of Foreign Affairs.

www.stmartins.com

Library of Congress Cataloging-in-Publication Data

Neven DuMont, Alfred, 1927–
    [Reise zu Lena. English]
    The diver / Alfred Neven DuMont ; [translated from the German by David
Dollenmayer]—1st U.S. ed.
        p. cm.
    Originally published in German as Reise zu Lena.
    ISBN 978-0-312-64798-8
    1. Older men—Fiction.   2. Daughters—Death—Fiction.   3. Fathers and
daughters—Fiction.   4. Marriage—Fiction.   5. Self-actualization
(Psychology)—Fiction.   6. Psychological fiction.   I. Dollenmayer, David B.
II. Title.
    PT2674.E28R4513 2010
    833'.914—dc22   2010037246

First published in Germany by Frankfurter Verlagsanstalt under the title *Reise
zu Lena*

First U.S. Edition: December 2010

10   9   8   7   6   5   4   3   2   1

Let my prayer come before thee: incline thine ear unto my cry;
for my soul is full of troubles: and my life draweth nigh unto the grave.

—Psalm 88: 2–3

The

Diver

one

The old man opens his eyes. Still groggy from sleep, he searches for a ray of light, the smallest glimmer. But the night has lost nothing of its deep darkness and keeps jealous watch over its gloom. And as he knows from last night, and the night before last, and many nights before that, he still has a long way to go, an eternity of waiting. Much too soon, blessed sleep has deserted him, throwing him back into loneliness. Soon the relentless questions will close in on him again, silent as bats on powerful, beating wings with an unerring instinct for the quickest way to their goal, their tiny heads and bulging eyes thrust forward. The same sharp pain again and again: Why did she go? Was it me? Was it my fault?

Then she's with him again. His heart thumps as he hears her bright laughter ring out, followed by the twitters and coos only she can make. When she laughs, he thinks happily, she is happy, released from the depths of her sadness. Released at last from weeks in that ink-black sea, she exultantly proclaims her freedom. Only someone who knows the endless, forlorn blackness—the unending plunge into the chasm of nothingness, the abyss that awaits us from which there is no return—can have such a bright, angelic laugh. His eyes blur and tears run down his wrinkled cheeks. He cannot speak. He hears a certain sound in the distance. His lips tremble. For a long time he clings to the apparition, won't let it go, won't surrender the lost happiness that has long since vanished. And he knows that he has fallen asleep again and been rewarded in his bitterness, if only for a short time. Time, that intangible, incomprehensible mass.

Is that Ann bending over him? He senses her face nearby. He thinks he can hear her breathing. Her eyes look at him through the darkness, observing, questioning, searching. She doesn't speak and he doesn't speak. Silence can last longer than death, he thinks. He turns his head to the side on the damp pillow and thinks of Gloria, his beloved daughter, and how she has just made his heart leap with joy in the middle of the night.

The old man sat up. His forehead was sweaty. His pajama shirt stuck to him. He shivered from the cold. Was it raining outside? Did he hear something? No, it was nothing. He swung his legs to the side, put his bare feet on the floor. He got used to the pains in his feet long ago. He didn't need any help—all that pushing and pulling, forward backward sideways, her cold hands on his shoulders, his arms, his back. What is he, a baby? No, God knows he's not. Just an old man. He thought, What have I done that I don't know where I'm going anymore? When did I lose my way? When did everything inside me get bogged down in endless questions and worries, senseless stammering? Why does this inscrutable God have no mercy? Why should he demand understanding, sympathy, forbearance, and compassion when he closes himself off from all such hopes? When he doesn't even acknowledge, much less reward, the humility I struggle to maintain day in and day out. What sort of a God is it who makes me his servant, his slave? My Lord, my distant master, not answerable to a single soul. Hasn't he ever heard me laughing in the night? He who punishes the innocent, the honest, and the devout and lets escape, unscathed, the dark, guilty figures—the drones, the flatterers, the facile, the secret thieves and sanctimonious murderers—or even rewards and honors them, gives them a place beside him at his table up above?

The old man walked through the garden with Ann. Her voice came to him from far away, as it often did, "Did you take your pills on schedule?"

His steps were quite hesitant today, his progress labored. He wobbled from one side to the other, stopped, then hurried on after her. Curious, he thought, is the garden getting bigger, or am I getting smaller? I think I am.

"Did you say something?" asked Ann sharply.

"Yes, darling. I think the garden is growing every day— getting bigger."

"No, you're wrong. The borders haven't changed for decades. We did buy a piece of land from the neighbors once. You wanted to plant a vegetable garden and some trees."

She walked at his side, straight-backed as always, a slim, stately woman not about to defer to anyone. She seemed to be growing, too. Would she soon be taller than he? Her face with its clearly etched lines, more deeply engraved with each passing year, severe, as if in the years and decades past one hadn't given her enough—he felt a pang of guilt.

"I remember two trees I planted, Ann, a cherry tree and an apple tree. The cherry died and the apple hasn't ever borne much fruit, I admit, but I think it's coming along. It just needs time. And then the vegetable garden: together we were going to—"

"Yes, that's right. But you left me in the lurch and I was on my own."

"You're right, darling, I didn't have the time. The company was insatiable."

"You allowed the work to devour you." He listened as her laugh turned into a deep, barking cough he thought would never end. Finally she said, "You were too good to your people. You got too involved with every single one of them. When you're the boss you have to put your foot down sometimes, like Father did."

"That was after the war. Everybody was in awe of his toughness."

"He was a model boss, a wonderful man. He wasn't about to kowtow to anyone. The Nazis made him pay a price for that, and it almost cost him his life. I was still a child but I remember at home we almost died of fear. The Gestapo came to the house, asked Mother questions, and once they took her away for a whole day. My sister and I and my aunt who'd been bombed out and lost her husband on the Russian front—we were all trembling for her safety. They'd already sentenced Father to death for his connections to the Resistance. He only survived because the Allies liberated us. My life began anew. He was my lodestar."

They had sat down on two wooden chairs, recent purchases of Ann's. He leaned back in his.

"Not everyone was as courageous as your father, that's for sure."

"Your family was more cautious. Your father was a fellow traveler and marched in their parades. He made accommodations, like most people."

Her voice had its sharp edge again.

He gestured toward the far end of the garden. "Look at that, the raspberry bushes are still there. They'll be blooming soon. You planted them when the children were still small, darling. We were eating raspberries for half the summer."

They walked slowly back to the house. A cold wind was picking up. The willow's bright green was the first delight of spring. Its thick roots ate their way deeper and deeper into the earth, then reappeared as new shoots. The root system spread out farther than the crown, overcoming the earth's crust with its thick arteries and then erupting again. He stumbled, quickly thrust his cane forward while his left hand clutched her for support.

He squinted at her, her body bolt upright as always. A soldier, he thought, a soldier. His Ann, perfect as always in her elegant, close-fitting cape over which she'd thrown a wide, light-colored shawl. Her hair bright silver, her lovely face uncommunicative. It wasn't really a mask, he thought. No, but there was something like a mysterious varnish spread over it, a protective coating.

"Did you take your pills?" she persisted.

Anton came over on Sunday with the children, his three blond boys. They ran to their grandfather, hugged him with their skinny arms, whispered something he didn't understand into his ear with their hot mouths, then disappeared into the garden like a whirlwind. Soon thereafter he heard Anton's deep voice scolding them.

"Get out of that pond right now! Immediately! You'll catch cold. Put your shoes and socks back on! Do you hear me?"

It was like hearing himself yelling. At Gloria. She's standing up to her skinny knees in the water, with her skirt hitched up and bending over to watch the fish. She pays him no heed. Her brows are knit. He says nothing more, otherwise she'll reply, "Papi, please be quiet! I'm sad."

Why hadn't he answered, "Me too, Gloria, I'm sad too. . . ." Perhaps that would have healed him, to say that to her. No one else would have understood, least of all Anton. Ann might have. But she was sick in those days. Her hip was hurting her— the operation, the long recovery—she needed his help. Why did I remain silent, never talk about myself? Yes sure, the business successes. It was easy to report good news: their wedding, Anton's birth and then Gloria's, the good grades they got— Anton did—the Order of Merit pinned to his chest by the prime minister, then that time in Greece when he pulled the little boy (his face was already turning blue) out of the sea and the mother kissed his hands in gratitude and made the sign of the cross on his forehead. And what about his doubts? His fears? His loneliness? Long ago, yes, at boarding school, he could talk to his friend Egon about them. They would pull their beds close together at night and lie there whispering to each other: one's mother hadn't written, the other's father was on a trip with his girlfriend. One couldn't understand the Latin homework, the math teacher hated the other. Luisa, his first love, a chubby-faced classmate asleep in the girls' dorm, hadn't looked at him but had smiled at another boy instead. Egon had died young. It had taken him a long time to really understand the loss. He needed a long time for a lot of things, too long to really understand them. Daily routine held him in thrall.

I just flutter around, he thought. No . . . I crash to the ground. I'm like a reptile, only looking out for myself, always just trying to survive. Is that what life is? He understood nothing. Now he tortured himself: It's too late now. Is it too late for me, old and sick as I am? It's very late, he thought. All is gone and forgotten.

In the dining room, his son sat down in Albert's usual seat and with a laugh directed everyone else to their places, beginning with the three boys. Who did Anton think he was, claiming the chair at the head of the table with such assurance when *he* had been the head of the family for decades, the paterfamilias? At some point, just once, in a fit of generosity, he had ceded the head chair to his son. It was a friendly gesture for that one day, nothing more. But Anton, endearing as he always was but not very sensitive, had continued to sit there Sunday after Sunday when they celebrated the family dinner so precious to Ann.

Should he say something? Not seriously, no, but more off-handedly—a little humorous remark? Not today, but sometime in the future, to put a stop to it once and for all. But he never got around to it. Anton was showing off today more than usual, playing the boss, talking about "my company" as if it were his and his alone and he'd been the one who'd built it up and made it strong. Even though his father—the predecessor and long-time head of the firm who had only ceded the position to him a few years ago—was sitting two seats away from him, eating his appetizer and taking his first sips of the Sunday Riesling.

Were his hands trembling again? Was that starting up again? He put them under the table, resting them on his knees. Don't get upset now, he thought, that will just make it worse.

"*Prost*, Anton!" he called out. "I've already had a taste. Nice to have you and the boys here. It's a great joy, a nice change of pace for Ann and me."

"What do mean, Father? You're the one who always puts so much store in tradition and family solidarity."

The old man could hear all too well the recrimination in his son's voice.

"It's a lovely way to honor the mother who took care of you . . . you and Gloria . . . so lovingly."

"Thank you," said Ann firmly. "Enough pretty speeches for now! And let's take life as it comes. We have to make peace with it . . ."

Her words grew indistinct in his ears.

He thought, I don't have to talk. It's not necessary. But I have to think of you, Gloria, I can't help it. Forgive me, dearest, for not leaving you in peace, the peace you so much deserve. But if you too refuse yourself to me, I won't know who else to turn to. Tell me, what shall I do?

Again, Ann's compelling voice rang out across the table, "Please eat, Albert. You're holding us all up. The children can hardly wait to get to the lamb."

Anton's inquisitive glance didn't escape him. The boys giggled. He said to Anton, "I hope you'll all come again next time! It's been weeks since Lori was here. She should make some time for us too . . ."

Anton seemed annoyed and not in the mood for jokes. The old man saw his wife's frown, the reproach in her eyes, her lips slowly parting to speak. "All right, Albert. Of course we miss her today, but we understand. Today's world has cast off our old-fashioned narrow-mindedness and replaced it with tolerance. Everyone has a right to their own fulfillment. . . . Let's not ruin this nice day, shall we? Let's be cheerful!"

That evening he was in the bathroom trying to unbutton his shirt, but his fingers had lost their strength and were fluttering wildly again. He sat down heavily on the chair that had been shoehorned into the cramped space just for him. His pants had fallen to the floor and were bunched around his ankles He bent down to free his feet, tugging impatiently at the pant legs until they finally gave in and he was holding the wrinkled pants in his hand trying to decide what to do with them. Should he get up, go into the dressing room, and hang them on the valet stand, or was it simpler to just drop them and undo the shirt buttons that were so uncooperative today? He heard her steps.

"But, darling, why didn't you call me? How was I to know you were getting ready for bed so early today? How many times have I told you I'm happy to help? You need me!"

He could hear the reproach in her voice. Ann stood next to him and had the shirt unbuttoned in a flash.

"I wanted to do it myself. I just needed more time."

"Admit that you can't do it alone anymore. It takes you forever!"

"It depends on the day. I don't usually need any help. I can handle things by myself."

"Why be so stubborn? Is it so hard to let someone help you? Don't be so pigheaded."

"What would you know about it?" he croaked, scratching his head.

She handed him his pajamas, picked up the pants, took his arm, and walked him into the bedroom.

"Why did you have to bring up Lori? You know very well how it hurts Anton's feelings. And in front of the boys . . ."

"Why doesn't he go get her back? I thought they were married." He was already lying down and Ann was sitting on the side of the bed.

"You have to understand. Times have changed. Women

today don't want to be put on display the way we were. Nobody wants to make sacrifices anymore the way we did."

Was that another reproach?

The old man stared at the ceiling. "Maybe you're right. We
men always thought of ourselves first. That's all different now.
Everything's changed. That's what you mean, Ann, isn't it?"

She stroked his forehead and gave him a weary smile. "Maybe
so, my dear. My life has just passed by at your side."

"I need to sleep now, Ann."

"You should sleep. I'll turn out the light and leave the door
open a crack, as always, so a bit of light gets in."

"I'm not a child."

"No, of course you're not."

His hand, calm and obedient, felt for the light switch, reached
over to the shelf, and felt for the notebooks: Gloria's diaries. The
old man passed a hand over his eyes. "Gloria, thirteen years
old," his lips whispered. His fingers glided across the wrinkled
pages with their awkward handwriting. The letters danced before his eyes. He could recite entire pages by heart. And yet
he read the entries again and again just as one never tires of
looking at a treasure again and again, with beating heart and
undiminished joy. There were some passages he was especially
fond of.

*Had a fight with Mami. She can be so critical sometimes. She
stepped on my left foot and I screamed. She claimed it was an accident. I don't know if I believe her—no, I don't believe her. But that's
just it: she doesn't believe me, either. It's not like it used to be. Later,
Papi came home. He came straight up to my room and comforted*

me, gave me a hug and kiss. He understands me. I'm so lucky to have such a wonderful Papi. My friends all think he's great.

And in the next notebook, when she was fourteen:

I got my period again, it's so stupid. It had to start on the weekend and Mami went to the lake to go swimming, typical! At first Papi didn't know what to do with me. Then we played a stupid game of dominos, but we laughed a lot, and later we played his beloved Ping-Pong. He tried to let me win but I saw right through him. Later he suddenly got sad. I think he's like me. He laughed in such a weird way—very brightly, and couldn't stop. Christie came over later and we slept cuddled up next to each other.

And then:

Summer vacation in Valais is the best, much better than Sylt. I don't like the ocean. I guess I'm afraid of the big waves. Once I was way out, too far from shore, Papi thought, and I thought I was going to go under. In the mountains we always have the same house, actually just a big log cabin where you can hear everything. For example, when Papi laughs you can hear it all over the house, or when my parents fight, which they always do on vacation. This time I was allowed to invite Christie. We get along fantastically. Usually Papi comes with us on hikes. He carries the rucksack and annoys us with his warnings to watch our step. But when we start talking about boys, he walks on ahead a bit. He's probably embarrassed. But I know he always keeps an eye on us. Our house sits a little above the village. In the next house down the hill, there's a family with two boys, towheaded twins. Unfortunately, Christie and I both like the same one. He's tall, has a cute nose and a cheeky smile. Really sweet. Papi has talked to their parents. They only speak French, so it's going to be hard for us when we go out to dinner together, as has been arranged.

He remembered that when they were driving back down after their weeks in the mountains, he looked in the rearview mirror and saw tears in Gloria's eyes. Her first case of lovesickness, as he thought at the time. Apparently, one evening she'd kissed the blond young man and then confessed to Ann that they were engaged—secretly, of course. No one must know! But Gloria never wanted to get engaged again, not even when she'd grown into a beautiful young woman. When he made cautious inquiries, she said, "No, no. Unfortunately not! It's out of the question in my case. I just wouldn't have the courage to get through it. Someone like me shouldn't even think about having children."

Not that she hadn't had opportunities, among others a promising young man who worked in the company. He would have liked to have him as a son-in-law. But no, she took life hard, too hard. On the other hand, her memories of their vacations must have been indelible. She always returned to the Valais even though she didn't talk about it. She found her way back there once more shortly before she died.

The next day, Erwin came to see him. For a long time now he'd been visiting him as a friend instead of as his doctor. Ann stood by the door as he entered the house. She hesitated a split second before she let him in. "I didn't expect you today."

He took off his coat. "Will summer never come? What an inhospitable place we live in!"

"What a nice surprise to see you today!"

He turned to face her and held out his hand. "You know I come every two weeks and always on the same day, if I can. I think your husband's happy to see me. He broods too much."

Lost in thought, she gave him a stern look. "You're right, and I'm grateful to you."

"No need for gratitude. As I've said, it's a pleasure to come as a friend. Your husband hasn't been my patient in a long time."

"A hopeless case, isn't that what you said? You didn't cure him, although you certainly had enough time to."

"No, I meant that in general, not about him specifically, but in general: a hopeless case. We're all hopeless cases. However, I look more for the hope that's present in every hopeless case. And at least we stabilized him and kept him from getting worse. Don't forget, he wanted to follow his daughter."

Ann walked ahead of him into the living room.

"I won't keep him waiting any longer. He must be expecting you. Black tea for you, too?"

She opened the door to the library, a narrow, high room with floor-to-ceiling shelves filled with books. The old man was sitting in a wing chair with his feet on a hassock and his lap full of books. Ann tarried a moment, watching the two of them greet each other warmly. Without further ado, Erwin pulled over a chair and sat down next to her husband. There was a tender smile on Albert's face. A smile he hadn't given her for a very long time, she thought.

"All right then, a cup of tea for the doctor, and you'd like another one too, I assume?" As she left the room, her movements were almost mechanical.

When Ann returned a few minutes later with a diminutive

tray and set it down on the hassock between the two men, her eyes were flashing. "But please, no dwelling on the same old problem again! Everything has to end sometime!"

"All very well for you to say, Ann," responded Erwin, "but at what point do you declare something over and done with? Many questions remain unresolved, sometimes your whole life long. I don't know of any formulas for answering them. But we'll try to follow your advice, dear Ann. We'll make an effort."

Now even Albert was laughing. "We'll make an effort, dearest. Don't worry."

She walked the few steps back to him and stroked his temples. "That's just what I was going to say to you."

Once she had closed the door behind her, the two friends sipped their tea and winked at each other like naughty boys.

"You can see she's trying, Erwin."

"Of course, but you don't make it any easier for her. You won't let her get near you or share your grief. You won't share. Gloria was her daughter too, after all."

"We've gone through all this so many times already, the eternal question I kept going over and over when I was your patient. How can you separate two people who have been married for more than forty years? Didn't she just say not to keep harping on the same old problem? And didn't you say we would try. So keep your word!"

"Albert, Albert, don't play games with me! Don't confuse the sorrow of losing a loved one with the topic of your marriage."

"You're right, Erwin. You've caught me out. But which of those is harder to resolve? You took the easy way out and got a divorce, you malingerer!"

"And suffered agonies, my friend, agonies! And afterward, it was worse than before."

"Serves you right!" Albert gloated. "There's a price to be paid for everything. But a psychiatrist who throws in the towel—that's surrendering to the enemy, isn't it? What kind of advertisement is that for your practice?"

"Touché! Congratulations! I have skeletons in my closet, too. You'll just have to live with them."

"I'm happy to live with them. It's a pleasure. It would be un-imaginably horrible, to have a perfect human being for a friend! You'd be right about everything—even more than you are already."

"Well, Albert, you love questions and I love answers. Is there a God? No, God is dead and we have to cope with things ourselves."

"By simply adopting his commandments as our own."

"I only meant to say that we complement each other perfectly. I let you have your biblical God and you let me have my Nietzsche."

They opened the wide glass door out to the garden. The rain had stopped and the sun was breaking through the clouds. They walked across the still-wet grass, looked at the flowers Ann tended so lovingly, and regarded the sky. They were seized by a rare sense of lightness. Albert walked behind his friend with small, hesitant steps but ignored his own clumsiness.

After Erwin had gone, the old man remained in the garden. With his handkerchief he wiped dry the bench farthest from the house, sat down, and listened to the birds who seemed to enjoy the sunshine as much as he did. The sound of music

drifted over from a distant house—probably a garden party—
with talk and laughter mixed in. To be sociable, he laughed too
and even clapped his hands in time to the music.

There's no reason not to be happy, he told himself out loud.
Gloria was grateful whenever they did something that made
her happy. It got harder and harder as the years went by. She
withdrew more and more, as if into a fortress she had chosen
for herself. Christie was the only person she allowed to be with
her. But God knows her loneliness was anything but her own
choice! She fought back tooth and nail, with increasing feroc-
ity. Hesitantly at first, but then decisively, she rejected any help
from outside. Her final, desperate attempts to escape: dashing
off to the Caribbean, the Cayman Islands, south to the Atlas
Mountains, north to the polar ice. Throwing herself desper-
ately into the arms of men from other continents. She clung
so hard to life, took what it offered, tried to keep her footing,
grasped at every stone and branch, even at the edge of the abyss.
And all to no avail. There was no footing to be had. Had she
really said to him, with a shy smile in her eyes, "You're the one
closest to me"? Had she meant it that way? But when she said it
she was still just a child.

He took a deep breath. The music seemed to grow louder.
The breeze carried it over to him. He clapped his hands again,
trying to match the rhythm.

What's wrong with me, he thought. Have I gotten entangled in her? That must be what Ann meant when she said to
leave her in peace! Didn't Erwin tell her we would try? Was he
talking more to me than to Ann? Ann needed no advice. She
was always so sure of her way! The first year of mourning was
long past, a second had followed, and a third was drawing to a
close. Some part of him had died with her. That's it. That's the

crux of it. I loved her more than I love myself. That's my failing: my self-indulgence. If that's so, he thought, then maybe
I'm mourning less for her than for the part of me she took to
the grave with her—the best part, certainly.

The evening sky had darkened; the distant music broke off
abruptly. He hurried back to the house.

What storm must I be on guard against, he thought, what
am I seeking shelter from? What did he, a sick old man, really
have to lose? Did he fear death? The thought was laughable.
Gloria had gone on before him. Wouldn't it be a joy to follow
her beacon? Then he would be free of the burden, the life that
oppressed and weighed him down. Gloria's loss was an invitation to an eternity almost completely elusive for him. At best,
he caught fleeting glimpses of it. But the body that housed
him—this old, worn-out body—was a painful drag. Had his
soul already gone on ahead, following Gloria, and what remained was nothing but repetition, ossification, loneliness, a
dead shell? With few exceptions, others viewed him as a leper
whose time was up, a spoiled article waiting to be recalled. Why
was he so bitter and resentful? No one had insulted him or done
him any harm. It was he who virtually invited those around
him—his family first and foremost—to treat him with indul-
gence and pity. And then they shared their concerns about him
behind his back. Gloria's death had been the catalyst, the shock
that was so hard to recover from. But the cause was deeper
and independent of it. What remained was himself as the af-
flicted one, his need for condolence, his plea for attention, all
wrapped in a fatal, impregnable pride that was completely, utterly unjustified. His former achievements—in business, soci-
ety, the family—if they had ever been worth anything at
all, were faded by now, evaporated like drops of warm summer

rain in the sunshine. The shining hero with a medal on his chest! Was that him? No matter: gone, squandered, over and done with. Who else would remember when he himself had such trouble cobbling together the pitiful remains of his past (to the extent they were still to be found) and presenting them once more to his family and himself?

That evening the two of them ate supper without speaking. There was cold fish and a salad with just a few sips of white wine in addition to water, with fruit for dessert. At last the silence was broken by Ann who seemed as self-absorbed as he was. "Tell me about Erwin. What's he up to? He seemed to be in good spirits."

"He is, and why not? We had a nice chat, nothing earthshaking. We've gotten past all that psychological stuff, thank God."

"Don't forget, there was a time not so long ago when he helped you a lot."

"If memory serves, he was *Gloria's* doctor for many years—her faithful companion, as he put it—"

"And couldn't fix anything."

The old man laid aside his knife and fork, straightened up in his chair, and took a deep breath. "I beg to differ, my dear. Many days he smoothed her path and dispelled her gloomy thoughts. Then *we* started consulting him too."

"*You* started consulting him, Albert. You needed him, not me. I know where I'm going."

"Fine, *I* did!"

Ann gave him a stern, almost ferocious look. "Results are what count, and he was a failure."

"In Gloria's case—in the end—yes, you could say he failed.

It was a defeat. Her longing to cross over was too strong. Even the best doctor is no match for the will of nature. How could he have succeeded when later on even the psychiatric hospitals couldn't do anything? But really, wasn't it our defeat too? It was mine for sure."

Ann had stood up. She was putting the dishes on the cart to be wheeled into the kitchen. "No, don't get up. It's easier for me to do it by myself. You always get a tremor if a glass or a plate falls and breaks, like a few days ago."

"I know. It was my fault."

Ann turned away brusquely. "It's always got to be somebody's 'fault'! My God, such trivialities aren't worth worrying about, are they? You have this illness just like many other people and I do all I can to ease your burden. But no one's at fault. If anyone is to be blamed for our suffering, it's God. And as everyone knows, God is without fault. The blame falls back on us humans. Those are the rules of the game. As it was in the beginning, is now and ever shall be."

Long before she was done he started to smile.

"You're talking about Christianity. If you go a little further back, the ancient Greeks were not so strict. Their gods mingled with mortals."

She called from the kitchen, "You're always either down in the dumps or making a joke out of everything, Albert. Can't you find a happy medium? Please, darling, it would make our life so much easier!"

He had gotten up and was standing in the kitchen door with his wineglass in his hand. He nodded his head slowly forward and whispered, almost inaudibly, "Yes, my darling."

"Hang on to your glass. I just remembered that Anton is going to stop by this evening. He wants to see how you're doing."

With his head still lowered, the old man repeated, "Yes, darling."

Ann was putting the packed-up leftovers into the refrigerator. "Talk louder; I can't hear you."

He returned to the dining room, carefully put the glass down, and although he must have heard the doorbell ringing, he continued on to the foot of the stairs, ascended to his bedroom, and closed the door behind him.

Before she opened the door and let Anton in, she called up the stairs after him, "I told you I couldn't understand what you were saying!"

Ann hugged her son tightly, clasped him in a sudden wave of desperation, tears in her eyes. "Oh, God," she stammered, "it's so hard! First Gloria and now him . . ."

Anton gently tried to free himself from her embrace, kissing his mother's forehead and her wet cheeks. "I seem to have arrived just in time."

"You're my only joy, the last one I still have," she sobbed. "I'm so happy you're here, you dear sweet boy."

Gallantly he took her arm and escorted her into the living room. "What's the old man been up to this time?" He laughed. "You know he doesn't mean it, Mother. Don't take every word he says so seriously! You know very well that Gloria inherited her depression from him. No trace of that in you that I know of. You're strong! I'm your child in that regard."

She sat close beside him on the sofa and stroked his left hand while her eyes shone up at him. "You have beautiful fair hair, such wonderful curls, and so thick. Who did you get them from?"

He laughed again. "Only you can answer that, Mother. It

must have been some handsome prince passing through that you couldn't resist. Who knows? You got married not long before I was born—giving rise to the legend of me being premature."

Ann sat up straight and smoothed her blouse. "Your mother is a decent woman! Now go upstairs and bring your father back down. He may be sulking, which he does more and more. Make him come down and be with us. You'll do him more good than that fawning shrink."

Anton took the stairs in a few bounds, stopped at the old man's door and knocked briskly. "Open up, Father! You don't have to lock yourself in—I came to see you. Can you hear me?" He put his ear to the door, strained to hear something. "Open up, please. I want to see you. We all want what's best for you."

Finally, he heard a voice from within. "Why not just come in? It's not locked."

Entering the room he could just barely make out the dim figure of his father stretched out on the bed. "Why are you lying here in the dark, Father? Or have you gone to bed already?"

The old man raised himself up on his elbows. "Take a closer look, my son! I don't usually go to bed in a suit and tie. Perhaps it will come to that some day, who knows, but not today. No, I just wanted to rest a bit and take the strain off my eyes."

"Are you coming down? Mother's waiting. We wanted to drink a glass of wine together."

Albert sat up, stretched his back, and took his son's hand. "Is that what we wanted? If you say so. And you don't think the two of you would rather be alone together? I wouldn't want to interfere. And you know, I've always got to be thinking about something. It's getting worse and worse."

"And you're just realizing that now, Father? You think too

much; everybody says so. You'll end up as some kind of mental millipede with so many legs you won't be able to find your way."

"You think so? But which 'way' do you mean? I don't understand. I don't know if I still have a path to follow. I feel I reached my goal long ago. I'm already there. Forward motion stops, of course. One turns in circles, sometimes happy, sometimes sad, like an old dancing bear in the circus."

His son took his hand firmly in his own and snorted with laughter. "What a lively imagination you have! But much too melancholy, not cheerful enough. Come along now! Let's go downstairs. Please, Mother's going to wonder what's keeping us. Let's try to be a little bit happy."

Albert gave a mischievous smile, "Okay, let's be happy! If you give me no choice, we'll be happy!"

Once they were seated at the table, the evening dragged on a bit. At his father's request, Anton had gone down to the wine cellar and come back with a bottle of Burgundy. The old man took the first taste. "We waited too long with this one! It's not at its best anymore. It's lost some strength, just a shadow of its former self."

Anton filled his mother's glass while she got out nuts and raisins. Then he took a big mouthful himself. "Nonsense! It's the same as always, no trace of weakness. On the contrary, it's wonderfully mature, just like Mother. Here's to you, Mother!"

They toasted her, clinking their glasses as in days gone by.

"You're a good son, Anton!" said Albert.

"Bravo!" cried Ann.

The old man lay in his bed, wakeful and restless. The lamp on the bedside table was still on and cast large shadows on the wall. Why can't I talk? he thought. Why this inability to communicate? Is it because I've become distrustful, because I feel like a convict? How did it come to this? Is it others' fault perhaps, Anton's and Ann's? Am I worried that they don't want to hear what I have to say? Maybe it will seem strange to them, abstruse, or worse: completely inconsequential, insignificant, laughable. Why am I afraid of being afraid? Why this inscrutable, fathomless fear with no concrete object? It's just there, meaningless, unsubstantial, without any way to pin it down. Or have I locked myself up out of pride, stupidity, lack of love? But I did love them, my daughter, my son. Should I go back downstairs and tell them the love is still there? It hasn't gone out yet. Let's bring it up from the cellar like that bottle of Burgundy that tasted so good despite—no, because of—its age. Anton said so, and Ann nodded in agreement. Will they laugh at me or snigger to themselves about the crazy old man and his strange notions? What if they do? What do I have to lose? Nothing, nothing at all! The wall of respect I constructed so carefully around myself lies in ruins long since. Its fragments evoke a weary smile at best. What did Anton—my only son, my only remaining child, my heir and successor—what's that he said to me on the stairs? "Let's try to be a little bit happy." What he meant was: Try to be a little happy, old man! Is that really too much to ask? Why so stingy? How about a modest sign of closeness, affection, a little attempt to understand? Do I really want to tell them: I'm alone in the world; I don't need you; go where you want—to the devil as far as I'm concerned; leave me alone! Didn't I tell myself that when I took leave of Gloria, I lost my fear of death? You only need to follow; she has shown the way. But if that's so, then why be grouchy, carping, suspicious? Why can't I enjoy my waning days? If the others have settled opinions about me, I may have shrunk to a mere grimace in their eyes. Why not shatter the distorting mirror they think they see me reflected in? Confuse them, show them something new and better! Flip yourself over like a hole card. Instead of the dreary, everyday back showing on the table, display the face: Look! The king of hearts! It trumps everything except the ace. If the ace is played, then and only then can you lower your flag and surrender.

He knew he would find Ann in the garden first thing in the morning. She loved the early morning smell, the dew that evaporates as soon as the sun comes up. The old man had woken up early and dispensed with his usual morning brooding and ruminating. Instead, he got up, put on his robe, and hurried out as best he could to find her in the garden. It looked to be a lovely day indeed, preparing to create the world anew after all the rain and low, dark clouds of the last few weeks. He walked in his bare feet across the moist grass, step by cautious step. Above his head, an airplane traced a wide arc in the sky. He heard the birds whistling and twittering and thought he saw a squirrel. His legs weren't working very well this morning, worse than ever. He halted and tried to calm down. The illness seemed to be taking its course. Finally he was standing behind her. Ann had her back to him and didn't hear him coming. She was squatting on the ground with some young seedlings lying beside her in the grass. She held a trowel in her right hand and in her left a hand rake she was using to loosen the earth. He bent down to her.

"May I hand you the seedlings? Maybe it will be easier to—"
She started and looked up at him. "Are you up already? Did

something happen? Please don't bother. It's better for you to sit on the bench and not exert yourself. You're not supposed to!"

"I'm not exerting myself. It's a pleasure to help a little."

A second, skeptical look. "For heaven's sake, what's gotten into you today? I hope you're feeling all right!"

"Why shouldn't I be feeling all right? It made me happy to look out the window and see you in the garden, my little woman already hard at work."

Ann struggled to her feet, put her hands on her hips. "I work hard all day long, what with the house, the garden, and you most of all, Albert. You and your illness keep me on the go. Have you noticed that? Or do you think everything takes care of itself?"

The old man stamped his foot lightly on the grass. "No, no. I think you're a wonder. I'm grateful to you. You take care of everything so well, like no one else can."

Ann straightened out her linen dress and gave a fleeting smile. "What I need now is a cup of coffee to recover from this morning surprise! Let's go inside. The flowers can wait. They won't complain."

He caught her by the arm as she started to walk on ahead of him. "Please, Ann, listen to me. I love you, do you hear? I love you!"

Distractedly, she freed her arm from his surprisingly strong grip, let her palm rest for a moment on his extended fingers, and then firmly repeated, "Let's go inside!"

The old man tarried a few steps behind her, thinking: What shall I do? She doesn't want me. She doesn't believe me!

Ann turned back toward him, and for a moment tried to soften her strained expression. "Please forgive me; I don't feel very well. I slept badly, maybe from too much red wine. Our illustrious son, that happy-go-lucky fellow, always keeps refilling the glasses."

Back inside, she sat down beside him on the small sofa in the library. She took several deep breaths. He knew she had something important to tell him. It was unlikely to be something pleasant; her face was getting more and more serious.

"Albert, you know Mary's written me twice lately. Early this morning, she called up. I could barely hear her she spoke so softly. She's back home from the hospital and it looks like they won't be able to stop the cancer. I also spoke to her doctor and he explained the situation in detail to me. It seems clear they're giving her up for gone. Her lung is all eaten up."

"Your poor sister," he interjected. "Shouldn't we go see her, the two of us, and brighten up her days a bit?"

She turned and gave him a searching look, "Do you really mean that? You think you could cheer her up?"

"Why not? You know how much I always liked Mary. What a charming young girl she was when we got married, always cracking jokes. Your little sister . . . remember?"

"Like it was yesterday, my dear!" Ann laughed. "You flirted with her quite shamelessly every chance you got. And you two danced together the whole time . . ."

"Yes, especially the waltzes. She could waltz like no one else. Leading her was like leading a feather. The way she could anticipate every move . . ."

"Albert, Albert, get a hold on yourself! That was forty years ago. Now your waltz partner is on her deathbed; her dancing days are over. The waltz ended long ago . . ."

His breathing was labored now. "I know, I know . . . and she's alone. But she's been alone all her life, hasn't she?"

"She never got married, if that's what you mean. We sisters

were independent women. That's how our father brought us
up. But she enjoyed life differently than me. Just think of her
string of affairs. After every one, she seemed to flourish and
just get more beautiful than before. Triumphant! She was the
first one of our circle of girls to talk about her men—holding
nothing back. She all but demonstrated her pleasure to us, enjoyed describing every detail. And her bedroom stories made
us married girls feel like stupid geese. We were terribly envi-
ous. I would never had been able to talk about things like that.
I don't think I would have had much to tell anyway. But now . . .
now she's paying for it!"

Albert got to his feet faster than he had for a long time. He
couldn't stay seated next to her. "You don't really mean that, do
you, Ann? There's no connection!"

She was sunk in thought, eyes closed. In a meek voice, she
replied, "No, you're right, Albert. Forgive me, Mary! My nerves
got the better of me. I got upset thinking about Mary as she
was back then. It must have stirred up feelings I've suppressed
and forgotten. She was a good person who lived out her passions to the full, openly, proudly. And she was rewarded with
glamour, beauty, and wealth. Remember Eduardo, the famous
tenor, and their tours from one metropolis to the next? And
then there was Heribert, the London banker—what a gorgeous
man! I didn't begrudge her that, Albert, please believe me! Do
you believe me?"

He sat down beside her again and took her hand. He slid
closer. Several minutes passed, then he heard her speaking again.
She had calmed down.

"Over, finished, forgotten! We have to deal with the present. I've thought everything through, planned it all out. I don't
think it's a good idea for you to come as well. I appreciate your

intentions, of course, and I thank you for them. But once I'm
with her, I should devote all my time to her. Don't be mad at
me, Albert. You need caring for too, but two patients at once
would just be too much for me. It's Mary's turn now. She's suffering more; she's the one at death's door. I've put it off long
enough for your sake, Albert. I didn't want to leave you alone
here. Now the scales have tipped in her favor. I'm leaving today.
I've taken care of everything. Faithful Irma has promised to
come every day. She'll do the shopping, look after the house,
and make you a hot lunch. She's also ready to give you a hand.
Besides her, there's Anton. He stops by every other day anyway, and I've given him a copy of the front door key. . . . And
then there's Erwin who lives nearby. It will only be for a few
days."

   He lowered his gaze. "Well, you've made your decision.
You're going to Mary's without me. I understand. It's a shame
there'll be no more waltzes."

Ann left at noon. Albert said goodbye to her in front of the
house. They hugged each other for a moment. He tried to re-
lax his arms and his torso; it was as loving an embrace as they
had had in a long time. Over her shoulder, he could see the face
of the cab driver, a friendly face with a three-day growth of
beard. The man watched the elderly couple hug and gave a little
nod. Albert thought he could detect a trace of empathy in the
driver's eyes—no, maybe admiration. The sound of the taxi's
engine lingered in the old man's ear for a long time.

   Then he ate the light lunch Ann had prepared for him. It
tasted good and he didn't mind sitting alone at the kitchen
table. He thought of Ann and how well she took care of him.

Could he make out all right alone in the coming days, even with Irma's help?

His afternoon nap lasted longer and was more refreshing than on recent days. His wool jacket hung on the chair. He lay upstairs on his bed with his belt unbuckled and listened to the empty house. His door was cracked open. The window to the garden was open too and he enjoyed the sunlight slanting in. He was overcome with an unfamiliar feeling: he was alone. No one in the house but him. No one would arrive or leave, no one interrupt his thoughts. Irma was quite taciturn anyway, hardly uttering a word except to ask a question now and then. And Anton? He was tied down in the office just as he himself used to be. He'd be glad if Albert didn't need his help. Anton, his son, who did everything better. Straightforward, consistent, success-oriented, the heir and boss, the heir of his grandfather, the founder. He, Albert, had only been a lieutenant, a stopgap, the son-in-law and prince consort, as they had already begun teasing him at the bachelor supper the night before he married Ann. He was convinced that he had been slower, less decisive, and more cautious than the position required. He had a hyphenated last name, had added his wife's to his own, as was appropriate to the situation but still unusual at the time.

While he lay in bed, almost weightless, he was also walking through the garden at her side. She smiled. "It's so nice not to fight."

"But I didn't say anything."

Silence. They walked in a circle, slowly, almost gravely, as if they were part of a procession. She stopped. "The lawn needs cutting. Your feet are wet. I'll let the gardener know."

She was standing behind him, looking intently at his back that is bent beneath his shirt. Lightly she touched his hair where it covered the nape of his neck, the way he wore it before they were married. She said it was too wild that way—too wild for the family business, for his parents-in-law.

"Your hair is so beautiful! I had forgotten."

Albert could feel his hands shaking as they always did when he got excited. He shoved them deep into his pockets. Ann, still behind him, laughed as she hasn't laughed in ages. She laughed almost inaudibly and for a long time.

"You don't have to hide your hands, my dear. There's no reason to hide your joy. And I'll let the gardener know . . ."

Her voice faded away.

"We don't need the gardener, dear Ann. I'll do the work. I can easily mow the lawn in two hours. I'll be done before you know it."

He turned around, but she has disappeared.

That evening, he fell asleep quickly. His thoughts had all fled. His head was on vacation. He slept through the night and more soundly than he had in a long time. The next morning he fumbled with his shirt buttons. He was putting on the shirt he had worn yesterday and there was no one to object. He considered whether to take it off again and put on a fresh one, as he should, or simply begin the new day in his old shirt. He could just wash his face and hands and brush his teeth. He didn't feel like doing more than that. He had gotten up early—earlier than usual—and it was just getting light. Wearing nothing but his old shirt, he went downstairs like a young man and poured himself a cup of coffee from the thermos bottle. The coffee tasted stale but he liked it that way. He sat a while in the kitchen, then got up and started wandering through the house. He pushed open the door to Ann's bedroom without knocking, looked around inside, looked at the photographs in silver frames: her parents, the children, the grandchildren, photos from her youth, of her sister and himself—their wedding picture!

The consciousness grew on him that he was alone in the house. Everything was different—it tasted different, smelled different and somehow new. The walls had pulled back and the ceiling was higher. He heard strange noises: the dripping of the kitchen faucet, the humming of the water heater. A child's yell was audible through the closed window. Everything was louder than usual. It didn't bother him. On the contrary, it seemed to make his solitude more bearable. He heard the squeal of brakes out in the street and opened the kitchen window. Had something happened? It's wonderful to have his kingdom to himself. He's the master of own time, eager for what the new day will bring. He will do what he feels like doing—maybe just sit in his easy chair in the library or on the bench out in the garden, weather permitting. He won't do anything. No one will disturb him. He'll eat when he's hungry, not at the appointed times. Maybe he'll eat less, maybe more. No one will be urging him to talk. He'll give the clocks a day off. No, he's not sick. He's a bit older—that's as it should be—a bit slower, but not sick. He would budget his strength. He'd get along fine, wouldn't have it any other way.

He wondered if Ann had slept well, how the train ride had gone with two stations where she had to change trains. He tried to picture his sister-in-law's pretty house on the edge of the small town where she had finally settled down at the end of her restless life. It had been too long since he'd been there. Her last beau, a retired professor, had inveigled her into moving there. The relationship had probably been a mistake. He was an upstanding, jovial gentleman of the old school, the sort you don't find anymore nowadays, but in the long run, he hadn't been amusing enough for her, and he'd died quite some time ago. Albert couldn't recall his face. Ann would call later and he'd hear about everything and tell her how much he missed her.

He straightened up his room a bit, recalling his student days. He'd often left his digs in a chaotic mess: the bed unmade, the desk overflowing with papers, books and notebooks all jumbled together, yesterday's clothes strewn heedlessly about the room, a woman's stockings still on the floor from the weekend. He laughed, tossed the books from his bed onto the floor where no stranger's stockings now lay. Downstairs in the library, he took a close look at the spines of the books. There were titles he didn't recall, books he certainly would never pick up again, others that piqued his interest. He took some of them down, read a few lines, and a new perspective on life opened up. And a look back as well: some older works that had seemed to stand the test of time now tasted insipid, others simply foreign. But he had neglected to do something yesterday, and he could and would make up for it today. He wandered into the dining room and sat down at his rightful place at the head of the table. He'd bought this table as a surprise for Ann on her fortieth birthday so they would finally have enough room for the whole family and their friends—enough room to feast a large crowd. Today it was quiet. He loved the quiet and allowed it to suffuse him. He stretched out in his chair with no one to challenge him. He rose, rapped on the table, squared his shoulders ceremoniously, placed his hands on the back of the chair, and regarded the assembled company. Silence all around; expectant, attentive faces. Everyone awaited his words with respectful curiosity. What would he say in celebration of this day? His words would lend significance to the banquet. Each person there would feel welcomed and personally addressed by his remarks that now commenced, slowly at first, deliberately, word by word, then flowing more freely, with amusing little asides for the children. He found his tempo. Salvos of words succeeded each other with pauses between, long pauses when the room fell so silent you could hear the breath of the person sitting next to you. People looked longingly at him: please, please continue! Don't keep us in suspense! When will you finally get to me, mention me—the exam I passed, my business coup, the child I'm expecting, my professional success? Albert meted out his praise and every recipient was thrilled by his formulations. He shook them up, questioned their doubts, gave encouragement, showed them the way. Finally the home stretch, the finish, played staccato, the stream of words ebbing away, his voice calming down, the end. He nodded his head slightly, modest and casual, and looked around with eyebrows raised in surprise as the applause swelled up, as Ann and the children and all their friends—Christie as well—released from his spell, jumped to their feet clapping, laughing, and cheering. What a masterly performance! Without a word he sat down again. It had been a happy day.

The front doorbell was ringing. A delivery? Maybe just some children playing a prank. Now it was up to him to open the door. To his great surprise, it was his daughter-in-law Lori. It had been too long, and he was glad to see her. She looked pretty in her summer dress. Her thin face still had the glow of youth, at least today it did. She had made herself up for him, without a doubt.

"I brought you something to eat, Father! Mostly fruit, some cookies—the kind you like—and a little salami to go with your special bread. I haven't forgotten! And a bottle of my favorite red wine from Italy. I hope you like it, Father."

Lori had never called him Father before; he hadn't forgotten. He sat in the kitchen while she made tea, sliced the bread, and put salami and tomatoes on it.

"This all looks delicious, of course. But most of all, I'm happy to see you, Lori. It's been such a long time. You look good, but a little sad around the eyes. Is something wrong?"

She looked down into her lap, stood up, opened the window, took a deep breath of morning air, wandered around the room, and finally looked him in the eye. "It's hard, very hard. With him I mean. He's very fussy. He won't allow any disagreement. He's getting bossier. I ask myself if it's just the business. 'I have to be the boss!' he says. But why at home, too? He still needs me twice a week in the Lutheran position, if you know what I mean, but otherwise he's not very interested in me. He's self-sufficient. And the worst thing is, he's taking the three boys from me. He's their be-all and end-all; they worship him. I'm just the housemaid."

Albert was silent. He stood up too, came over beside her, and put his arm around her shoulder. "And do you think I could— be of some help to you? Should I talk to Anton, open his eyes?"

She gave him a timid look. "That's not why I came. I'm here because I wanted to see you again and . . . because you're . . . you're the only one in the family who understands me, now that Gloria is gone."

For a moment she leaned her cheek against his. The long

hair he'd always liked so much tickled his ear and nose. Is he allowed to be happy? He is happy. So I'm good for something after all; I'm not alone, he thought.

Once they'd sat down again and were sipping their tea, she told him that she'd gone back to work. Her pediatric practice was going better than she'd dared to hope. Just before she left, she said, "If it's all right, I'll come back soon with a surprise visitor. You'll be happy to hear that Christie got back to town a few days ago. She's brown as a berry from the African sun. Working down there has rejuvenated her. Helping others must be good for you, especially the poor. Compared to her, I feel like an old woman with my problems."

"Oh, come now! You're in the prime of life, no question about it. It's a good thing you're starting a new life. You have so many wonderful things to look forward to, I'm sure of it. You just have to want to . . ."

"You really think so? You make me so happy—more than you'll ever know!"

She pressed the old man against her warm body and for a moment he thought he would lose his composure.

Christie was Gloria's best friend, her lifelong companion, her closest confidante. She was the sister Gloria had never had. When the girls were children, everybody loved Christie, even Ann. She was a part of the family. Later, it was hard for Ann not to be jealous. She was bothered by the two girls' closeness, their blood sisterhood, and their secrets. She felt she was standing in front of a door that was locked against her. Anton however, the big brother, adored his sister's friend who stayed over as often as she could and slept next to Gloria in bed. He loved her often boisterous temperament, her wildly unruly hair, her bright bursts of laughter. But he didn't stand a chance either; the two girls were too exclusively involved with each other. Anton felt like a fifth wheel in their company and also felt neglected by his father. But for Albert, the house shone with the reflected beauty of the two girlfriends. He saw their happiness and welcomed it into his soul. It was the most wonderful gift he had ever received. He had so much experience of life's shadows that he was taken unawares by this sudden beam of light. Then it lasted so long that when it was abruptly extinguished, he was plunged back into even greater darkness. He had never recovered from the loss that pierced his heart.

Albert lay awake a long time that night, thinking. He couldn't get to sleep—didn't want to. The news of Christie's return to the city had given him a jolt and opened up the old wound that had barely healed. He had failed, and Christie had fled because she couldn't bear the calamity any longer. She had thrown herself into a new mission far away: taking care of children, the elderly, and the dying in Africa. Now she had returned unexpectedly with no advance warning.

It brought the Valais back again! Albert himself had set them on this path with his love of the mountain air and the expanses of high, snow-covered peaks. Gloria shared his passion for their mountain village at a time when hardly any outsiders had discovered it. Anton had gone his own way early: camping in Brittany and conquering the Greek islands. Ann put up with the Valais, playing bridge with French ladies in the little inn where they liked to have supper. And so during the day, he had the mountains and the girls to himself. They would often bound up a mountain ahead of him, like goats, challenging his strength and ignoring his warnings to be careful. Their skirts billowed in the wind, revealing slim brown legs.

The more Gloria's illness came to dominate her life, the more she sought sanctuary in the village of her childhood where she still found something resembling peace. Sometimes she brought a man along, but like everything else, those episodes never lasted long. Sometimes she came with Christie. Then her trips to the Caribbean began. She learned to scuba dive. And that is where the tragic end came. More and more, Gloria had closed herself off from him and everyone else and in the end, he lost her. She showed up at home less and less often. She said she had to go her way alone. And he couldn't or wouldn't understand what she meant by that. Who was with her on her final journey? Was she alone? When she died, was someone there at her side—a boyfriend, some stranger? Death by drowning! Wasn't she an accomplished swimmer and enthusiastic diver? As he finally learned after endless inquiries, she died with all her equipment on and the oxygen tank on her back. Christie called with barely a word of explanation about how it had happened; thereafter it was impossible to get in touch with her. Christie, the intimate family friend, failed just when they needed her most. Had she lied to him? More than two years had passed but it still seemed as terrible to him as if it were yesterday. Now he was an old man and had to struggle greatly to accept his life as it was before it was over.

In the middle of the night, he woke up and looked around in bewilderment, rubbing his teary eyes. He must have fallen asleep with the light on. The room was still brightly lit. Slowly, he raised himself up and sat on the edge of the bed. His legs felt numb. The old man could feel his face assuming a stern expression.

Not like this, he thought. He wasn't going to end his life like this: humbly, thankfully accepting the charity of the Good Lord, cringing and cowering in awe. Fury crept into his skull, invaded his limbs, shook his entire body. He jumped to his feet, grasped his head in both hands, looked angrily toward the sky.

He was driven restlessly through the house. As spryly as he could manage, he made his way from floor to floor, throwing open the doors of the little mansard rooms under the eaves where the children had had their bedrooms. Everywhere he went, he turned the lights on. He wanted the whole house ablaze with light from top to bottom; he would drive out the gloom, the pervasive darkness in the rooms around him. Yes, he would do so once and for all.

The old man raised his voice, stronger and louder until his bellowing reached the last corner of the house. "I quit, effective immediately. I'm revoking my contract because of deceit—malicious deceit—fraud, misappropriation—misappropriation of my life—because of malice and capriciousness, but most of all because you took away the dearest thing I had to gratify all the more easily your greed for another victim! I accuse you of manslaughter, of perfidious murder! My suffering is your joy. You expect humility and devotion in order to use us at your pleasure. Your hands are stained with our blood, your mouth smeared with it. You are more ravenous and violent than the most fearsome beast. You allow humankind to tear itself apart, man against wife, mother against child, brother against brother, son against father. The nations fall upon each other at your bidding. You incite one against the other, drive them to a fever pitch of fury, despair, fear, and blindness and they butcher each other in a pit of broken bodies, slick with sweat, wounds agape, fertilizing your earth with their blood, and its stench rises to heaven like a poisonous bubble for your delectation and delight! Yesterday there were thousands, today there will be millions, tomorrow tens of millions. Now as in the past, you put into the hands of your creatures, your children (long since stepchildren), the playthings of death. First it was lances and spears, then sabers, rifles, and cannon, then missiles—through the air, under the sea, on the land. You stand by while they acquire more and more tools of death for your pleasure, pile them up like a hoard of gold and diamonds, gaining dominion over the whole earth and arming for the next attack. And in the end, the great hour will be at hand: the great, incomparable, unparalleled bomb, created by a genius who resembles you and atomizes all life on earth. Countless millions will die, humans of all colors, animals of all kinds. Gigantic cities filled with skyscrapers will collapse like a house of cards and bury everything that breathes. Vast swaths of land will wither and die or be flooded by raging waters that open new seas and sweep innocent children, unsuspecting women, and grandparents into the abyss. The dying will proceed east and west, north and south, until at last the earth is again what it was at the beginning: without form and void. Humankind will have vanished! But don't forget: you will die with us. It will finally be achieved: all of us, all humanity, will be the victims, but we created you, just as you created us. We created you and your prophets, both the honest ones and the hypocrites. Like the toadies of a despot, they will share in your fall. Peace, longed-for peace, will reign at last for all eternity! Didn't Moses himself say, 'If thy presence go not with me, carry us not up hence?' And so it shall be at the end! Worth the price of the doom we will share, hallelujah, hallelujah, hallelujah! You said, I am alpha and omega, the beginning and the end!"

Exhausted and gasping for air, Albert sat down on the stairs. His hands were trembling. "Once you were in me and I in you. You became the world, but the world didn't become you. You allowed us to resign from the covenant. You transformed yourself into an alien god and every evil ran its course."

He sat slumped forward with a heavy head, as if drugged. Yet with each passing minute he became more and more suffused with an unfamiliar feeling of happiness. Although his limbs were trembling, something like a ray of light fell across his face. The blood pulsed more quickly through his arteries and his body glowed with heat. He had dared to do it, dared to speak it! He had rebelled, carried out a successful revolt. Yes, it had happened! Was he free? He hardly dared to say it. He felt like a long incarcerated prisoner whose chains have just been struck off. Could it really be true? Was this reality and not some treacherous dream that would soon thrust him back into his accustomed dungeon? No, through his own strength he had liberated himself, not the Almighty! There was no doubt: he had done it himself. The happiness within was not ephemeral. Or did the cunning one up above have his hand in the game after all? He couldn't accept that it was so. No one could cast doubt on his victory over himself, no one on earth or anywhere else.

He got to his feet, climbed the stairs to the second floor leaving behind the brightly lit rooms, and lay down on his bed, weary but happy. Almost immediately, he fell into a deep, sound sleep.

Albert spent the following days in a state of semi-intoxication. It had been a long time since he had ventured out of the house. To go with his summer suit, he took care to choose a checked tie (although the knot ended up a little askew) and donned the Panama hat purchased years ago on a cruise. The low garden gate squeaked as he opened it; the hinges could use a few drops of oil. The young trees lining both sides of the road—maples if he was not mistaken—were progressing well. Here and there, a house had been freshly painted. The pretty little homes turned a friendly face toward him. Albert stopped to admire the flowers in their front yards: roses, tulips, daisies, even lavender. We'll have to get busy if we're going to keep up, he thought.

The newly installed wooden bench at the corner was a welcome chance to sit down. There was already an old man sitting there who returned his greeting with something like a grunt or low growl, but even that couldn't dampen Albert's good mood. He took a good look at this neighbor sitting there with a stooped back and his hands resting on a cane, lost in gloomy thought. Two or three cars glided past, shiny red and blue in the morning sunlight.

"Nice day, isn't it?"

The old man didn't move, and no reply was forthcoming, but Albert wasn't ready to give up just yet.

"The sun feels good after all that rain! I think this weather's going to last, don't you?"

His neighbor didn't seem to hear. I wonder how old he is? Maybe just my vintage, thought Albert as he slowly got up, leaning on his own cane—the cane with the sterling silver head that Gloria had given him. He only used it on special occasions.

"Sorry to disturb you. Enjoy your morning!"

He was already turning away when he caught the almost inaudible but bright voice behind him, "Same to you!"

He turned back and said, "Perhaps we'll see each other here again!"

He saw the old man's face: lined, wrinkled, the eyes small above swollen features.

A hard nut to crack, he thought.

The little neighborhood grocery around the corner had managed to survive despite supermarkets not far away where customers could stuff their trunks full of purchases. In this neighborhood there were mainly retirees, but also young couples with children who would be in school at this time of day, leaving the narrow suburban streets in almost paralyzing silence. As he entered the little store, he was warmly greeted by the elderly Mrs. Huber, whose name he fortunately recalled.

"What a surprise to see you again! We haven't had the honor in quite a while."

From his pocket he took the little list of the most important things they needed, written in Irma's legible hand. In addition, he asked for peppermint pastilles, dark chocolate (which he hadn't had in quite a while), and a fairly good cognac he happened to spot on a shelf, and returned home with a well-filled shopping basket. From the bench where he had rested a short time ago, the other old man watched him pass in silence, his hands still resting on the handle of his cane. But Albert thought he could catch a nod of his head, and there may even have been a shy smile on his face. Back at the house he sat down in the library and put his feet up on the hassock, exhausted but content. The telephone rang. It was Ann.

"What are you up to, Albert? I've abandoned you and I can't help worrying about you all the time, but it's worse here. I should have come sooner than I did, God knows; sorry, but you're going to have to do without me for a few extra days. I think my poor sister is near the end; it's going faster than expected."

Albert took a deep breath, "I miss you, my dear, but don't worry about me. I'm managing just fine."

"Irma said you'd gone out alone to shop. She was so excited about it—in her own prim way, of course, with just two or three words—and even thought it was due to her care, the good soul. . . . But what I wanted to say is: I've hardly left the house and you're doing something dumb and irresponsible. Imagine if something had happened to you on the way to the store! God only knows it's not fair to me, and at the very time when you should have some consideration for me, when I'm tied down here with my dying sister!"

Albert stayed calm, studied the ceiling where the previous owner of their house had installed genuine plaster molding.

"Don't worry. I'm rationing my strength."

"I also heard about Lori, I mean about her visit. You should have kept out of that, as I told you to . . ."

Albert was silent at first, then, "Nothing happened that you need to worry about. And don't worry about me, either."

Ann was crying and almost inaudible as she hung up. He could just hear her sobbing, "It's too much, too much . . ."

What was going on? Something didn't seem right. Where were his grief, his pain, his despair? Something had obviously happened overnight; at the very least, he had been granted a reprieve for an unspecified length of time. By tomorrow, it might be all over and malign habit would suck him back into his old hole more quickly than he had left it. Involuntarily, he recalled his first trip to America. For days on end, he had walked the streets of New York and Washington, D.C., as if intoxicated, all cares behind him. And then, after unbelievably happy days, he had turned back into the same old worrywart as before. It was as if he had lost his shadow and then it caught up with him again. But now, today, he threw back his shoulders and walked through the world without a care, released from his weighty burden. It was sunny even when the sun wasn't shining. He smiled. Everyone was smiling. Even the grumpy couple next door waved back at him. He got Irma to talk more than she had in years, a miracle in itself. She told him about her doctor's appointments, her back pain, her swollen feet. As best he could, he gave her advice.

He began to write in his diary, that very morning. His handwriting was small and scrawly. He regained possession of his waking hours and even his nights seemed less foreboding. When he awoke in the dark, he told himself calmly, "Soon it will be light." He left the lamp on his night table burning until dawn. He began listening to music again: Bach, Schubert, Brahms, Mahler, Stravinsky, but also popular things on the radio. He took a taxi to a shop that sold CDs. It had at least doubled if not tripled its floor space since the last time he was there. He caught himself singing along with a Mozart opera. Irma overheard him and stifled a laugh with her hand, her eyes twinkling.

Erwin stopped by. "I wanted to see how you were doing all alone here. It must be hard without—"

"Without Ann, you mean?" the old man interrupted him. "Well, Ann. When you live with someone, you get so . . ."

"Used to each other?" Erwin supplied.

"Something like that." He had to force himself not to show his hand too soon. Let his friend talk.

"Well after all, my friend, you're ill. I know how it is plaguing you more each day, and differently from one hour to the next. Sometimes it really hits you hard and then other times it seems to just disappear."

"It is insidious, that's for sure! And you think I need help? Don't worry, I'm getting along fine by myself. I don't need anything."

They stepped out into the garden. Erwin matched his pace to Albert's. With great gravity they strolled side by side across the lawn. Although it was starting to turn cool already, they sat down on the old wooden bench among the shrubbery. From there they had the best view of the house in its pretty setting between the bright green willow and the lovely white trunks of the birches.

"That sounds suspiciously positive." Erwin laughed. "And what else do you have to report?"

Albert smiled back. "What do you mean?"

Now Erwin was grinning. "How should I know if you don't?"

"Talking about things doesn't always make them better. I think I already talk too much about myself."

"Do as I do: don't think about anything."

"I've heard that before, but it's very hard. Okay: it's nothing, it's nothing, it's . . ."

His friend looked at him expectantly. "You know, sometimes I have doubts about my profession. The older I get, the more I recognize that it's almost impossible to help people. I can't bring their story to a halt, stand fate on its head. The best I can do is change their consciousness. We know our spouse, our family, our friend, our colleague. We know them all well, perhaps our enemy best of all, but we know ourselves the least.

You remain forever a stranger to yourself. You want to solve the riddle, but without success. It's a funny feeling to realize you've been going through life in the body of someone you don't know and may even have wrong ideas about."

The old man slapped his thigh with a palsied hand. "Forget about God and it's a step in the right direction! Once you get rid of that triangular relationship, you can start to make some progress. Then there's just your stranger and the person you think you are. It's easier to have a discussion with just two people. You get to know each other better, you're not so ashamed that beneath your clothes, you're naked and have to admit that your body wants something different from your head."

Erwin stood up and faced him. "What's gotten into you? Were you struck by lightning? Or have I corrupted you with all the Nietzsche baggage I carry around?"

They resumed their walk in the garden, Albert leaning on his friend's arm. Darkness was slowly falling. Erwin came to a stop and took Albert's hand. "So now all of a sudden you think God is dead?"

"Everyone has to decide for himself. But surely the thought isn't new to you?"

"I don't know, I just don't know. Even if God has been dead for quite some time, I still always feel there's something there. Call it a source if you will. It's a surrounding presence, anyway, whose breath lasts far longer than ours."

"And can you pray to it?"

"You're in an ironic mood today! At the risk of annoying you: yes, I could pray to it in an emergency."

"There are no atheists in the foxholes, as the saying goes! You forget about him, lead a happy-go-lucky life, and then when you need him—presto, he jumps out of his box. Pretty pathetic, don't you think? So he's a sheet anchor for somebody who's lost his way, a God in reserve."

"That's how I think of him, anyway. What about you?"

"Okay! If it has to be that way, then I agree, but only as long as I can revile him and judge him as he judges me."

Erwin burst out laughing, "That makes you an apostate: a pal, God as your pal! You've gone a good deal farther than me."

Albert joined in the laughter, "Too far you mean, right? And then comes the abyss . . ."

"Amen! I think it's time we went down to your wine cellar."

They sat in the library, the old man in his wing chair and Erwin across from him on the small black leather couch, each with a glass in his hand.

"Albert, I think you're pulling my leg. Tell the truth: have you been praying?"

"If that's what you want to call it, yes."

Later that evening, Albert sat watching TV. The news was about to come on. The newspaper he'd already read lay in his lap. Unexpectedly, Anton entered the room, bringing the coolness of the late hour with him.

"Just a short visit, Father! You remember Mother gave me the house key so I could look in on you any time?"

"That's right, Anton. But please have a seat. It makes me nervous when you march up and down the room. You haven't even taken off your raincoat."

He turned off the TV with the remote control just as the news was starting. Anton let his coat drop to the floor in a heap and threw himself down on the leather couch.

"I see you're feeling well, Father. You look splendid. So I'll get right to the point: you invited Lori over, showed her a lot of sympathy, gave her an affectionate hug like she was a good, loving daughter."

Albert looked intently at his son with just the trace of a smile on his face.

"That's right. Lori was here. But she came to visit me. Should I have shown her the door right away?"

Anton jumped to his feet again.

"Father, you seem to want to treat this as some sort of joke. But I'm in no mood for fun! Our Lori, who's hardly spoken a word to me for some time, has been puffing herself up in front of me and the boys, boasting loudly about the marvelous, friendly, effusive welcome she got from you, full of empathy and understanding for the poor, unfortunate wife whose family— and especially her ruthless spouse, your son—treat her so badly. A quote from you. The father: a darling of a man; the son and husband: a son of a bitch!"

Anton's face was flushed and he threw himself back down onto the black couch that groaned beneath his weight. Albert still regarded him attentively, but his continuing silence fanned Anton's pent-up resentment into anger.

"Well? What have you got to say for yourself, Father? Why don't you say something? You've delivered a stinging slap in the face to your only son; you're stabbing me in the back in the midst of a serious crisis in my marriage—a crisis that Lori and Lori alone is responsible for. Really stabbing me in the back . . ."

Albert sat up straight in his chair, carefully took his hands from his thighs and calmly folded them, looking at Anton the whole time.

"So, I'm waiting," his son finally burst out. "I'm all ears."

"Me too," said the father after another pause. "And first of all I would suggest that you calm down, Anton. I have a certain amount of sympathy for you: the constant business pressure you're under, your family duties, and much else . . . you're over-extended. But I think you can't expect good results from the way you're currently running your life. And now my answer, short and sweet: I have nothing to say in my defense. Of course I treated your wife, whom I feel just as sorry for as I do for you, in a friendly way. That's the only way I can help your shaky marriage. And another thing: I didn't stab you in the back. You're not sure where to turn. That can happen in a marriage, and I admit there are extenuating circumstances. However—and this is the most important thing I have to say to you—you've got to solve your own problems, settle your conflict with Lori, heal your rift. No one else can do it for you."

Anton furrowed his brow and finally answered his father. "Fine. I've listened to your lecture, listened patiently, as usual. But I don't find it convincing. On the contrary! You feel sorry for me, you grant me extenuating circumstances—what a travesty! That's the way you treat people you expect sympathy from for yourself? Most unfortunate of all, you seem not to acknowledge that you should be on my side. You play the judge, expect me to recognize you as such—aloof, emotionless. It's hard for a son to accept that his father's going to leave him in the lurch just when he needs him—very hard. But maybe I'm expecting too much of you. Mother complains about you too. While she's worried sick about you and her sister, you're putting your health at risk irresponsibly. You're acting foolishly, burdening her with new worries when she has more than enough already. Isn't it about time, old man, to stop thinking about yourself and start thinking more about your loved ones?"

Anton was already in the doorway. Albert hurried after him, chuckling, "I'm trying to, I'm trying . . ."

It was early morning and Ann was already calling. Albert was still in bed when the shrill ring echoed through the house.

"Yes," she said weakly. "I didn't sleep well, only about two or three hours. No, you shouldn't take everything I say so literally. Taking care of her is wearing me out more than I expected. And I'm coming to realize more what you mean to me, my dear. That's what I wanted to tell you so early in the morning. Can you hear me, Albert?"

He cleared his throat, "Yes, yes, of course. That's sweet of you, and nice to hear. Thank you! Ann, don't you think maybe I should—"

"No, absolutely not! I've got things under control here. Just think, now she's blaming herself! She thinks she got so sick because of the kind of life she led. And she used to be more beautiful than any of us. How we envied her! Now she regrets all those men she threw herself at—her dissolute life, as she calls it. She says there was a lot she didn't tell me or Father. I'm so exhausted. I can't persuade her that it doesn't work that way. What do you think, Albert?"

"Are you asking if I think the body will rebel when the soul is damaged, suffering, when it's been thoroughly suppressed? Perhaps it's possible . . . but you can't prove it."

He heard Ann take a deep breath on the other end of the line. "Didn't we have a book about that? A scientific theory, with examples? I wanted to bring it along to Mary's but I couldn't find it before I left. Do you have any idea where it is?"

"You bought it because you wanted to find out if there

might be a connection between my illness and way I lived my life."

"It's important to find out if you've made some mistake. I wanted to be fair to you, too. As fair as I could be."

"What I heard was more like a reproach, a complaint that quickly turned into an accusation."

"My dear Albert, I don't know what to say . . . what do you mean?"

Agitated, he was pacing back and forth in his bedroom. "Well, if you must know: I threw that book into the trash weeks ago!"

"Into the trash? You don't usually . . ."

"Do such a thing? Is that what you were going to say? You'd be surprised at all the other things that belong in the trash."

He heard her breathing again, louder this time. "I'm very upset. What are you referring to?"

His voice grew sharper, "I just mean we need to get rid of all our excess ballast. Even old people have a right to live, don't you agree? We drag so much old baggage around it's enough to suffocate us! Wouldn't it be great to make a fresh start, Ann?!"

There was a long silence before he heard her voice again. "I'm tired. I don't think I've got the strength to . . . I just don't understand all that. I think I'd better lie down and rest a little."

Albert had barely calmed down when Christie was at the door. He'd had an awful night, slept badly, tossing and turning and dreaming he couldn't fall asleep. Having that false dream was more oppressive than endless insomnia. His head was muddled: hideous faces appeared to him, repeated laughter, and then a persistent drumming that hurt his ears. The sound was still in his head when he woke up, but finally the drumming came to an end.

He was having his breakfast of coffee and toast with honey when Irma showed Christie in, followed by Lori. They came into the kitchen. Albert was taken aback—how could he ever have forgotten Christie? But it was Lori behind her, not Gloria. Was this a temptation? Was he being lifted up only to be dashed to the ground again? Were these devils or demons sent to tempt him? Or had a demon already taken up residence inside him, and he just hadn't admitted it yet?

Christie didn't look like the success story Lori had made her out to be. She was pale and seemed hesitant and ill at ease. They greeted each other with a hug, but it was tentative, almost incorporeal: two beings who had thought about each other for too long now looked over the other's shoulder. Catching Christie's mood, Albert had struggled out of his chair, and was still having trouble shaking off Anton's visit last evening and his telephone conversation with Ann. Now he and Christie were at a loss for words. They all went into the dining room and sat down at the big table, perching somewhat uncomfortably on the high-backed chairs, as if waiting for a conference to begin. Lori spoke up first.

"Well, Father, here she is at last, the heroine of the Dark Continent. I had to twist her arm to get her to come, even though I know very well how much she likes you."

There was another painful silence while Albert and Christie reached for the water glasses in front of them and each took a quick swallow. Albert couldn't shake off his sluggishness—on the contrary, it got worse. Lori's words seemed to go right past him.

"It's amazing all the stories Christie has to tell about Africa:

the enormous distances, the endless, wild, uninhabited land-
scapes. And then the people, jammed together in miserable conditions: birth and death and war and persecution. She's seen it
all firsthand: epidemics where not just sexual contact but any
contact at all can turn into a deadly nightmare. She's told me
about crazed dictators and death squads that wipe out entire
ethnic groups, generals who order the devastation of whole
swaths of country so it's easier to starve out the population—"

He heard Christie's unpleasantly shrill laugh and recalled
the drums in the night. Then Christie spoke in the voice he
recognized. It reminded him of Gloria's, only hoarser, huskier—
smoky.

"Whoa, Lori! What's gotten into you? It's taken me days to
tell you all those things, and now you're pouring it all out in
just a few minutes! Be a little more sensitive. Tell Albert about
the flower I found in the desert, the fairy-tale flower I discovered in the real world. Tell him about the miracles I saw—the
eyes of the children, the woman I cured of her long illness, the
infant laughing in my arms."

Albert's hands fluttered uncontrollably as his fingers tried
to brush away the tears obscuring his vision. Under the table,
the soles of his shoes clattered involuntarily on the floor. It
sounded like well-fed rats scurrying furtively back and forth.
He felt Christie embrace him from behind, felt the warmth of
her body. The pressure of her hands upon his shoulders intensi-
fied, became unrelenting. Not until that moment did it become
real that Christie was finally there, after so many years, bringing
a piece of Gloria with her, only a wisp of her, perhaps, a beam,
a covert glimpse. Now his tears were flowing freely, a waterfall
that blinded him. How wonderful it was to let them run their
course, to lose himself and forget his trembling hands, his

clattering shoes. The old man lay on the sofa in the library, not knowing how he'd gotten there. Maybe the two women had carried him over. Had they grunted under his weight? Lori wasn't in the room anymore. She must have left the house already. What would she tell his resentful son this time? Maybe he would come by again. But he wouldn't dare cause trouble when Christie was here. His pent-up male indignation would melt away at her hoarse, husky laugh.

And then the thought was there, striking him like a bolt of lightning: the question that had tortured and plagued him since Gloria's death, the question he was unable to ask Christie, didn't dare ask her, the question that had consumed his soul ever since, whose answer he hoped would release him from his own bitterness, the question about Gloria's final hour. Christie and Christie alone had the answer. Gloria's final hour!

Christie was curled up in his armchair. Her eyes seemed to be closed. Her face had gotten thinner, almost translucent. Her body was delicate, bony, like an adolescent girl's. And yet it was neither a girl's body nor that of a grown woman. Perhaps it was the body of someone who had lost herself, misplaced herself somewhere. Her chest rose and fell. Was she asleep? Sleeping in his armchair, that grandfatherly old piece of furniture he'd inherited and had re-covered several times? It was reserved for him, almost a part of him, too big for that skinny female body, which it almost swallowed up. He was looking at her as she opened her eyes.

"I shouldn't have come, I know. I frighten you. The past—it's still so near when I'm here. Gloria is still here. Why don't you let her go, Albert? They say we should leave the dead in peace,

don't they? Then we can be at peace ourselves. I know now why I went to Africa. I went to forget, to let go, to start a new life, to find new hope. Without that we would suffocate."

"And did you find it?"

"Yes, yes I did, finally. . . . It was hard in the beginning, the first few months were pure torture. Every single day I wanted to go back, be with her, even though I knew she wasn't there anymore. But at least to be near her places, breathe her air—here, but especially up in the Valais where we were so carefree and happy. You were, too. I wanted to smell the earth, plant flowers, lie down in the meadows in the sunshine. But then reality finally caught up with me: the laughter of the children, the sick who looked to me with such desperation, the eyes I had to close. Every day, every hour, many nights. You change, lose yourself in a larger world where people are freer than here, less preoccupied with themselves, less subject to fear—because God is closer, I think."

Albert sat up, ran a hand through his hair.

"And now you're here! Wait a little, give me some time, and soon I'll be happy. And I think you're not that little girl anymore who came to the mountains with us. You're not Gloria's twin sister any longer, her shadow in good times and bad. Now you're the woman from Africa, the Good Samaritan. I'm an old man and Gloria's been dead for two and a half years."

Christie stood up, smoothed out her dress, stretched a little. Her body seemed to grow larger, her hair to regain the sheen it used to have. He remembered it. It was almost the same color as Gloria's. You could hardly tell them apart, the little girls' hair tousled together when they lay in each other's arms in bed, asleep already, not knowing what was in store for them.

She walked to the window and looked out at the garden.

"Look, it's started to rain. In Africa, that's always something special. It's like the whole garden has been dipped in water. Water! You have too much of it, and down there we have too little. The world is unfair."

"No walks through wet grass? What a shame. You could go barefoot."

She turned back toward him.

"You're still living with one foot in the past."

"I think about the past a lot, about the two of you, about how you told me I had to treat you like young ladies starting right that minute. We laughed a lot back then. I remember that. I'm permitted to remember, aren't I? At the end of your life, you look back. I recall many things from my boyhood better than what came afterwards."

He looked at her. How changed she was—a woman, a beautiful woman despite the lines in her face and her serious expression. It felt like he hadn't looked at a woman in a long time.

*Later they sat down to lunch. Irma, clearly pleased by Christie's presence, had bought some fish. Albert asked her to bring a bottle of white wine from the cellar. When Irma had gone home, Christie took his hand. The wine had softened her voice.

"I thought about it a long time before coming to see you. I've been back quite a while already—more than a week. I'm staying in the country with my mother. It was high time. You were like a father to me, Albert, a foster father. And for a foster child, a foster father is perhaps even more valuable than a real father. A child can't ever lose its father, but a foster child can. She has to always draw attention to herself if she wants to be loved and not forgotten."

"I remember so well how lively you were. Sometimes I thought you wanted to outdo Gloria."

"I yearned for you, for the father I never had—worse than that, for the father that would make me forget my real father. And I wanted to be like Gloria and put my arms around your neck. You can't imagine how often I was consumed by jealousy of her, of your love for her, of your unspoken mutual understanding and your secret glances just between you two. I had to outdo her with my love."

"I remember you showing off your long legs to me. You even asked if they weren't the most beautiful. Another time it was your hair. You wanted me to admire you."

"And in the end, you were as excluded as I was. I knew you were desperate and helpless. Gloria wanted to spare you and probably hurt you worse in the process. I was aware of what we were doing to you. Uncertainty is terrible! I was sure you blamed me entirely! That's why I ran away head over heels— from you and from her long shadow that held me in its grip. I didn't even pack properly, couldn't say goodbye. I arrived down there with nothing but lipstick and a suitcase full of books. The books were useful at least. It was a long time before I found my place. The worst of it was that at first, I understood nothing, not even myself. But I gritted my teeth and got down to work, lost thirty pounds so that men stopped looking at me entirely. I didn't even notice. Fleeing Gloria was also a flight from you. I knew you would never forgive me for not saving her, for my utter failure. I was too weak. I couldn't tell you—tell you what it was really like at the end. My inability to prevent Gloria's fall. I could neither look you in the eyes nor bear the thought that I would lose both my beloved sister and my father as well."

Albert had lain back down and stretched out his legs. His

breathing was labored and his gaze wandered across the high ceiling again.

"Your love for me that you talked about—wasn't it worth telling the truth? You sold me out. You both sold me out. But you were in your right mind and you . . ."

His voice died away. They remained silent as darkness fell. Albert seemed to have fallen asleep. She sat on the floor by the window. She heard his voice from far away: "Leave now. I want to sleep."

The old man awoke in the middle of the night, the sound of his own quavering voice in his ears.

"Why won't you allow me into the exalted circle of your mercy? Why do you refuse me that? Am I still in your debt? Why does my liability keep growing when I'm trying so hard to pay it off? Sometimes I feel on the brink of inner bankruptcy. You indict me, but I believe in you. Whoever doesn't believe is cast out. And I ask, I plead with you to let me enter your dwelling place, to give me permission to die. She was the one thing I loved, much more than I loved myself. You took my life away but left me to go on living. You took her from me because you wanted to have this angel for yourself. A goodness for which I should be eternally grateful to you? But I won't lie to you: I'm not grateful, not one bit. And I'm unable to perceive any mercy behind your curse. You see, for your mercy I'll give you my truth."

He got up from the sofa, half asleep, and padded upstairs through the brightly lit house. Leaden weariness weighed him down.

When Albert woke up the next morning, it was already

light. Suddenly he felt more refreshed than he had in a long time. He tossed the blanket aside and discovered to his surprise that he was completely naked. Who had undressed him?

Gloria and Christie went their way without me, he thought, without turning their heads in my direction. They always strung me along, but when it turned serious, they cut me out. They had no more room for me. Why was he only seeing that now, when it was so crystal clear? They had gone their way, and now he must go his, alone, without them. That simplified everything. He felt good—a new beginning. He went downstairs in his robe without taking his usual shower. His step was firmer than it had been in a long time. He clapped his hands, seeking a melody.

The breakfast table was set for two. What did that mean? He gave Irma an inquiring look. She made a sour face, gave him a hostile stare. "You want to know what happened? We have a guest and you let her sleep on the floor. You didn't even get out a blanket for her. That angel sacrifices herself for the poor and the sick down there in Africa and you live in the lap of luxury. I've got to tell you, Herr Director, that I don't much want to stay in a household like this!"

Albert stared at Irma in astonishment. Never before had she let loose such a tirade. As he sat down, she gave his chair a demonstrative shove against his legs and slammed the coffeepot onto the table just as Christie entered the room, almost without a sound. You could see she had just gotten out of the shower. Her hair was still shiny with moisture. Albert started to get up, but she gently pressed him back into his chair and sat down beside him, looking bright-eyed and wide-awake.

"I'm sorry—I didn't realize you were still here. I thought you left last night. I must ask your forgiveness."

She pushed back her hair. Irma, still angry, stood behind her.

"I don't mind sleeping on the floor. I'm used to it—it happens all the time in Africa. I didn't want to leave you alone. Now I've showered. Let's not let Ann know I invaded her bathroom."

"Although you waited until Ann left to come by," Irma interjected suspiciously.

"Yes, that's right. I wanted to talk to you alone, Albert. You know Ann and I have a difficult relationship."

While they ate Albert's toast and sipped their coffee they could hear Irma rattling around upstairs. Albert listened intently. He didn't know what to say. Christie smiled at him.

"Well, you look rested. Did you sleep well?"

"You do too, Christie."

"Strange, after the evening we spent together."

"Yes, strange. . . . You could just as well have slept in Gloria's attic room. You know the way, after all, and the bed is always made up. Maybe you'd like to . . ."

Christie took his hand. "No, I'm not going to stay another night. I've got other things planned for you and me. Listen, I want to take you with me today—really! And no argument! I've only got a few more days in the country and we should make use of them. Who knows when we'll see each other again! We'll pack up a few things and drive out to our place for a few days, out in the country, where Mom lives. The country air and all that nature will do you good. And best of all, quite apart from the change of scene, we'll have a chance to talk! It will be a welcome distraction for you."

"No, no, I couldn't possibly."

She had taken him by surprise, but he wasn't convinced. Albert couldn't even remember the last time he had spent a night away from home. One trip to another town to go to a museum, a visit to a restaurant on a special occasion, the annual Christmas Eve mass, and two or three times to the philharmonic, that was it. Anton had driven them out to his hunting lodge in his big car, but Ann had always insisted on returning to sleep in her own bed at night. It had been years since they'd gone on vacation; Ann was afraid he would overdo it.

And what would Ann say about this? She would be appalled. No, he'd couldn't subject her to that. She had enough to deal with right now as it was. Such were the spirited objections he raised.

But Christie was not to be gainsaid. She insisted on the plan that had formed in her mind. She was determined. She swept aside any further discussion, rose from the table, and went upstairs with Irma, who was obviously in on the plan, to pack his things.

"I know just what the director needs—better than anyone else," Irma declared.

While he remained glued to his chair in vain protest, Christie called down from the second floor, "Any special requests? A favorite sweater or anything? We've packed the toiletries you need and your light shoes. Your walking shoes are already downstairs ready to go. If there's a book you can't do without, you'll have to fetch it yourself. Otherwise, there's plenty to read out there. You just have to put on something appropriate. Shall I help you?"

"That's the last thing I need!" he scolded from his chair. But finally his curiosity drove him upstairs. "You're worse than Gloria in her best years, Christie! And now, out of my bedroom, ladies! Give an old man some privacy!"

When he came back downstairs, his suitcase was already in

the front hall, along with his coat, hat, and walking shoes. Still somewhat bewildered, Albert sat down in the kitchen again and took another swallow of the now lukewarm coffee.

"Christie, this whole mission is your responsibility. You give me no choice. If I come along, it's under protest and under compulsion. I'm being abducted."

"You'll enjoy our little outing to the country all the more for that!" She beamed.

The old man looked up at her.

"Well . . . if it makes you happy! It looks like it does, at any rate."

And after another swallow. "What shall we do about Ann? I can't just sneak off."

"Aha, Herr Director needs permission from the lady of the house, even though she's not even here," piped up Irma from the front door, Albert's suitcase already in her hand.

"I've got to get in touch with Ann right now, or there'll be the devil to pay!"

"It's comfy down there with the devil. No one freezes to death." Christie looked around for the telephone and found Ann's number.

"Maybe it doesn't have to be right now. We could take a little stroll in the garden and calm down. We could talk everything over . . ." he backpedaled.

"No, you have to do it now, this minute!" Christie insisted. "I've already dialed her up for you." She handed him the cordless phone.

"My God, what are you doing to me? From the frying pan into the fire!"

After two or three rings, Ann answered. Albert shooed the two women out of the kitchen with his hand.

"Hello, Ann. I just wanted to check in. . . . How is Mary? . . .
What did you say? There's a buzz in the line. . . . I understand.
You've got to stay a few more. . . . You already said that. Poor
Mary! . . . No, no, I understand completely. Everything's fine
here. Of course, I miss you taking care of me, but . . . what? No,
nothing special. You said you called Lori? That's news. . . ."

He strained to hear; now her voice was clearer: "Yes, Albert,
I talked to her. . . . You gave me the idea. I thought a lot about
everything you said to me. One has to see both sides, isn't that
what you said? Lori told me about Christie, too. . . . Has she
come to see you yet? Was she nice to you? She owes you at least
that much, God knows."

He was on his feet now, walking back and forth in the
kitchen.

"Guess what? She wants me to drive out to the country with
her to visit her mother, just a little excursion for a day or two.
What do you think of that? . . . What? It's up to me? . . . You
mean, if it'll do me some good? . . . Of course, I'm being well
looked after. . . . She sends you her best. . . . Yes, she's gotten
more serious. Living down there leaves its mark on you. . . .
Give Mary a hug; you two are always in my thoughts. . . . If
you think so, I guess I'll . . ."

Albert ended the conversation nodding his head, then went
out into the hallway where the two women were waiting.

"I caught her on a good day! Poor Mary, what a charming
young woman she was! And how she could waltz. . . ."

He watched the ever-changing cityscape fly by. They soon
reached the river and crossed the town along the water. The
trees lining the avenue had been recently pruned. Christie took

the bridge near the cathedral, drove through attractive suburbs, then past workshops and abandoned farmsteads. She crossed a highway and left the built-up area behind. She drove efficiently, sitting there beside him, and told him about her life in Mali, where she'd been stationed for almost a year now. Yes, of course she'd visited the legendary Timbuktu, but that goal of so many Sahara travelers wasn't such a golden place anymore. Far from it: today it was a filthy hole, half devoured by sand—as she put it—with animal droppings all over the dusty streets. A place surrounded by desert, where time had stopped long ago, a place in which you forget where you are.

The old man was enjoying this unexpected outing more and more. They'd already passed the large forest and the cemetery with its never-ending walls. He didn't like cemeteries, those museums of the dead. He would never have had the strength to visit Gloria's grave if there had been one. The landscape outside the car opened up into rolling hills. He liked going uphill best. At the rise, groups of trees appeared, the occasional chapel, villages with half-timbered houses to the right and left, in between a gorge, then more smokestacks, low-slung factory buildings—a thriving country, he thought, no need to worry! Occasional blue sky, then thick white clouds high up. Somewhere in the distance, rain was falling.

They must have been driving for an hour already when Christie pulled over on a hilltop to enjoy the view spread out before them: broad patches of forest interrupted by fields, some already harvested.

"We'll be there in just a few more minutes."

She opened the window to let in the fresh air. He took a deep breath.

"This is the life, by God! The air smells so good!"

In the far distance they could make out higher ground, a mountain range.

"I could keep driving like this forever, maybe all the way to Africa! Count me in! I'd forgotten how beautiful the world around here is."

Albert had put his arm affectionately around her shoulders. He looked at her with gratitude.

"High time you took me on a trip, Christie. I've been waiting a long time for it. You won't get rid of me so easily now."

The house was smaller than he'd expected. It hugged the ground and its roof hung so low he could reach it with his hand. The building was gray with green shutters peeling their paint. You could have overlooked it where it stood, at the edge of a large meadow. The compact property was enclosed by a hedge of tall bushes and a few old trees. The only remarkable thing were the roses, climbing the walls of the house and wherever else they could gain a foothold. Everywhere, hedges of them were in bloom. Christie's mother was obviously a rose lady. The roses cast a spell over everything else.

Albert had never been to this house nor had he seen Christie's mother for what seemed an eternity. He couldn't remember exactly when the last time was. Now here she was, coming toward him through the gloom of the entrance hall, bashful apparently, small—much shorter than he remembered her; Christie was more than a head taller—and somewhat stout, in a faded linen dress and clunky shoes with mud clinging to them, her wavy gray hair combed back. But with a full-lipped, lively mouth.

Is she embarrassed? Albert thought. Perhaps it's awkward to have me here.

Behind him, Christie said something he didn't catch and her mother answered. She seemed to be apologizing and he didn't know what for. Why would anyone need to apologize to him? He thought of Ann with her tall, ramrod posture, so full of self-confidence and sense of duty, her finely chiseled features becoming sterner with each passing year.

"I have to thank you for letting me come along. I'm sure Christie had the best intentions; I only hope I'm not a burden. I'm a pretty useless fellow."

In the living room tea was ready for them. A tea light was burning beneath the pot. It was a tidy, low-ceilinged room that made its inhabitant, as she led him in, seem even shorter and stouter. He liked the simple furniture upholstered in natural fabrics, the old rolltop desk on one wall, and the squat lamps.

"No, no. It's no trouble at all to have you here. Bringing you along was the one thing Christie wanted. I hope you'll help me persuade her . . . uh, what's past is past . . . I know how much you mean to her; you can influence her. But right now, we'll take your suitcase to your room. It's not much of a room, actually, more of a chamber you'll have trouble turning around in, you're so tall."

The day ended in silence. He went outside with the two women to explore the surroundings and breathe the air. They walked across pastures and a little way into the woods. He stopped to admire an anthill almost as tall as himself, larger than any he'd seen before. His steps got shorter and shorter, but he didn't want to give up. On the way back, he had to stop often to catch his breath and he leaned on Christie's arm.

In the evening the fire blazed and crackled in the fireplace.

The three of them sat watching the flames flare up and die down. They spoke only now and then. The lovely, eventful day had tired Albert out and his hands were shaking. He asked their permission to retire early. Without waiting to be asked, Lena unbuttoned his shirt for him and knelt down to untie his shoelaces. He was touched and didn't try to stop her. He lay in bed in the semidarkness, stared at the wall just beyond his feet, where a large child's drawing hung. A masterpiece, he thought, as he dropped off to sleep.

two

Albert rubbed his eyes in bewilderment. How was it possible to wake up in a strange bed far from home and yet be so happy? He had slept long and soundly, untroubled by bad dreams. His secret fear of being overcome by confusion and desperation anywhere but in his accustomed lair had vanished overnight. He had taken a contemplative stroll in the garden, inspecting the plants and flowers and peering up at the trees. Now he was sitting beside Lena with his hands folded and his legs crossed and resting on a cushion. Christie pulled over a hassock and sat down nearby. Last night she had announced that she was going to read to them from her notes—as she called her diary. Her mother and Albert would have to indulge her and be patient: her voice was husky and strange-sounding this morning. She was obviously struggling to stay calm.

Mother has asked me to write down my story. She thinks it will help me gain clarity about my life. For a long time I didn't want to do it and ignored her suggestion. But in the last two years, I've had a lot more time on my hands. Under the night sky of Africa, the questions come unbidden: Who am I? Who are my parents? What did Gloria mean to me—the sister who wasn't my sister? What does my mother mean to me—the mother who's not my mother? And the father who wasn't my father? And what about Albert? Why all the lies, the false hopes, the expectations of what real life would be solely on the

strength of my immoderate belief in them? And they did become my life until the dubious and fragile nature of my in-
vented world sadly and painfully caught up with me.

What is my reality? Is it my mother, the biological mother
who didn't want me and gave me up? Or is it my second
mother—you, Lena—who took me in as a child and loves me
as only a mother can? Is reality what people call "real life" or
is it what I feel and think? But what if I feel and think things
but my blood—what I inherited—wants something else? How
can one live with such conflict, such shame?

I know I've been running away from myself my whole life. I
always wanted to be someone else. I was led astray, let myself
be seduced . . . by Gloria, my sister, my twin, my blood sister,
my über-sister! Worse: I wanted to be Gloria myself, Gloria the
Second—even Gloria the First—I wanted to beat her! I wanted
to become one with her. I loved her with every fiber of my being, with every hair on my head—my hair that was so much
like hers. I wanted to be as beautiful as she was, only more so.
And I wanted to be loved like she was, to trump her whenever
I could. I wanted Albert to love me as much as he loved her. He
was our first beau and we competed for his affection; at least I
did so, with constantly redoubled effort. What a triumph it was
for me when I got a good-night kiss from him in Gloria's presence! I fell blissfully asleep, having gained eternal salvation.
It's high time to tell you, Albert, that I was pretending. To be
Gloria's sister and your daughter I lied to both of you. I'm not
the person you think I am.

Christie held her manuscript up close to her face as if hiding
behind the paper. At first she read hesitantly, paused often, but

she was reading quickly and fluently by the time Albert interrupted her.

"I don't want to hear this!"

"But it's true, Albert. And you need to know it. I was pretending so I could be your daughter. But I'm a different person."

The old man had stood up. He walked unsteadily through the house, bumping into things along the way as if he'd lost his sense of balance. He went out into the garden and stood there although a light rain had begun to fall.

Taking him by the hand without a word, Lena fetched him back to the house. Then went to look for Christie. She found her pacing restlessly back and forth on the narrow terrace in front of the house. "You scared him away," she said to her daughter. "He doesn't understand."

"It's what you wanted," Christie answered. "You told me to write down the way it was, find the truth—my truth."

"I didn't mean it that way. It's you I'm concerned about—you need to find yourself. That's what I told you when you left me helter-skelter to go to Africa. That's all I said."

"It was obviously too much for him. He doesn't want to hear it."

Later, Lena was busy in the kitchen and Christie came into Albert's room.

He was lying on the bed and humming to himself, holding his fingers up to the light and playing with them. "After Gloria's death, it felt like all my memories that had anything to do with her had been wiped out. I don't mean to disappoint you, but you were important because of your friendship with her. I never looked on you as a daughter."

His voice became quieter, almost inaudible. "When Gloria died, I didn't banish you from my life. I always loved having you at our house because you were such a big help to us. But then, in the end—yes, I blamed you in part."

He didn't hear the sound at first. Then he turned his head toward her and saw that she was crying. Albert sat up, concerned, and continued to gaze at her. "I'm sorry. I didn't know what to do with my pain. It was unbearable. Talking to Ann was impossible! Every word withered on the vine before it was even uttered. We would pass each other like two helpless strangers. I needed someone to blame. My pain, which kept turning into anger, had to fasten onto something—anything. I suppose it's human nature to find a scapegoat! Then we think justice is being served. What nonsense!"

After a while he repeated, "I'm sorry."

Christie took hold of his hand. "She was precious to you."

"She was my miracle! I always wondered how I could possibly have had a daughter like her. Her beauty, her charm, her whole being were almost otherworldly. Did we deserve such a child?"

Albert swung his legs off the bed and laughed out loud. "My God, listen to us! We're slinking around like ghosts, disembodied spirits. I've had enough of playing ghosts now. Enough! To hell with all this humbug!"

Christie stood in silence, looking pensively out the window.

"It's stopped raining. Maybe we'll get some sunshine this afternoon."

"Then let's go into the darkest part of the forest and hang our ghosts. We're dragging an overloaded bag of them around with us. We're nothing but little cripples, about to collapse under its weight. Let's get rid of them! Throw them away! Will you help me do it?"

Christie took his hands and pulled him up until they were standing face-to-face. She took him in her arms, hugged him tightly. She realized she hadn't had a man in her arms for a long time. "What's wrong with us? I think I'm getting dizzy. . . ."

"You're dizzy too? Why should it be any different for you than for me, Christie? Life doesn't play fair."

The gate leading out of the garden was just a few steps from the front door. The wooden fence that enclosed it was covered with vines and didn't even come up to Albert's waist. They crossed the dusty country road leading to the village and walked along a narrow path lined with blackberry bushes. Beyond, to the right and left, was a sea of high grass and wildflowers: dandelions, daisies, and poppies. Two or three hundred steps farther on rose tall dark firs. Christie went first, Lena took up the rear, and Albert walked between them as if under their protection. Circumspectly, the silent threesome approached the forest. One could have mistaken them for a group of conspirators with something up their sleeve. But Albert was only seeking a knotty tree trunk, dripping with resin in the darkness of the forest, on which to hang his bag of ghosts.

They found another anthill even bigger than the one yesterday. Albert was fascinated by it. Where are they heading, running back and forth and up and down without end? At whose behest were these tiny, nimble creatures under way on their scurrying legs—thousands and thousands of them? Their paths crisscrossed each other, trailed off into the distant forest, and then up the sides of the lofty anthill, with millions of minuscule fir needles stacked on top of one another by the huge slave army, as if by magic. They were bringing more and more needles; where would they all go? Would the hill become ever higher and larger? He, the all-powerful human being, could put a brutal end to this swarming activity with a single blow; with a big stick he could interrupt their work, rip open the million-headed colony, invade, destroy, trample their cells underfoot by the thousands. No one would take him to task or drag him into court for it. He, a multiple—no, a mass murderer—could take revenge for the misfortune, the offense perpetrated against him, with a surprise attack on this innocent colony. He could take revenge, unburden himself.

He shivered. A forest swath led down toward a clearing. On the right was a raised stand for hunters. Should he climb up there and wait for deer to show up? They stepped across a gurgling stream that had worn a bed in the forest floor. Still in their initial formation, the threesome crossed a slope and reached a narrow, gently descending valley. Albert stopped. His legs were unsteady. He stumbled over to a nearby tree trunk that a storm had brought down and sat down. The two women sat beside him.

"I'll stay here until it gets dark! I'll lie down over there in the moss, where the sunlight is sparkling. You can come get me tomorrow morning if you like. But if you forget, that's okay too. Then I'll forget myself and finally have some peace."

Lena laughed. "He's right. We've dragged him much too far into the woods, Christie."

"It's just his ghosts, Mother."

It was a long way back. Albert was exhausted and his steps got shorter and shorter. Often he had to pause for breath. Every bench along the way was a welcome sight. It was already dark by the time they passed the giant anthill again. He leaned first on Christie's arm, then on Lena's, who almost had to stand on tiptoe to help him. At the edge of the woods they took a short-cut down to the road, hailed a passing car, and asked the driver to give them a lift. Back at the house, the women got him into a tub of hot water to regain his strength. Albert let them take care of him, even allowing Lena to help him get undressed. She's my nanny, he thought. Not a word was spoken. Back in his room, he fell deeply asleep for an hour, then woke up feeling reborn. Late in the evening, they ate a light supper. Albert drank his first swallow of red wine eagerly. After a short silence, he turned to Christie. "And now tell us your story. I was unfair to you when I interrupted you before. Tell it from the beginning. Tell how it was. Please . . ."

"All right. You two have a right to hear it. And I have a right to see my life clearly." Christie had the manuscript on the table in front of her and began to read from it again.

The first thing I remember is a beard: a big, black, frightening beard belonging to the man I thought was my father. But when he bent his face down to mine, it didn't just instill enormous respect in me, but something else as well, something that was hiding in his eyes, or better, behind his eyes and flamed up from time to time: love. Mother Lena was always there, her hands, her breath, her body. I can recall it clearly. Unlike my father, she was always there. Often when I looked into her face, she dropped her eyes, as if from shame, as if plagued by a bad conscience whose source I couldn't know. Sometimes I was afraid she was trying to hide something, that there was a secret she was keeping from me. Many things dropped away over the years, but a shyness toward me remained. As I got older, however, my doubts were slowly laid to rest.

Our lives passed without much excitement; we lived quietly, monotonously even. Father was a strict, churchgoing Catholic and said the blessing before every meal in a powerful voice. At times, we thought we could hear some reproach in it. He never missed church on Sunday, and although he was anything but gregarious, his status among the congregation grew from year to year. I think it was due to his beautiful tenor voice, which floated so beautifully above the others in the church choir. There is no doubt that he was an imposing man, always in a dark, conservative suit and black tie. He loved being in mourning. Whenever his work allowed it—in my recollection, anyway—he was hurrying from one funeral to the other, even if he were only slightly acquainted with the departed. He was especially eager to attend if he knew that only a few mourners would be following the hearse. Because of his impressive appearance—you could easily have taken him for a mayor, a famous preacher, or a school principal—a funeral with Father in attendance was an event. He lent it significance and dignity. Father was no principal, however, but just a simple high school teacher. He had no ambition for higher office, categorically refused any promotion as incompatible with his religious beliefs. He taught German and history and was respected by his colleagues and feared by his students. Or so I thought at the time. It was a rude awakening to find out much later that there was no teacher the students razzed so much and made such malicious jokes about as my own father. This painful discovery filled me with sympathy for him as I grew older.

We didn't talk about feelings in our little family. It was strictly taboo to address each other with kindly, loving words. It was all too easy to expose yourself to the charge of being talkative and engaging in flattery—in other words, of saying something vain and dishonest that could easily slide into committing a sin.

I never saw Father wear anything but his dark suit. Even at home in the middle of the summer, he only took off his jacket when the heat became too oppressive. Once, carelessly, I bumped against his chest and arms and started back in shock. It was like bumping into a skeleton. He must have been nothing but skin and bones. In the seconds it took to bump him and then jump back, he shot me a hostile look. I was only twelve. Henceforth we dealt with each other more and more like two strangers.

In the summer we never went swimming together like other families, neither at the town pool nor at a lake. We took just a few days' vacation, usually somewhere in the far north. The very idea of free and easy enjoyment of nature was never even considered: it was a frivolous distraction, Nor did I dare ask permission to go on a similar excursion with friends. Thus, my image of my father had hands and a face but no visible flesh. I heard him tell my mother that sin was of the flesh and that one must conquer one's body with the spirit. Such was God's commandment. As a child, I understood that statement no better than I did his repeated assertion that sin originates in woman, who must be on her guard against wantonness. Eve was held up to us as a warning. She must have been a brazen hussy. I never saw my mother undressed either, not even in a bathing suit. Her skirts fell well below the knee and she too increasingly preferred dark colors. Mother saw to it that at home and especially outside the house, even at the height of summer, I was always completely clothed. When someone had died, even some distant relative I had never seen in my life, I had to put on black—to the malicious delight of the other girls in my class who made fun of our family, the "eternal mourners."

All the more reason why I recall so vividly two incidents that happened during my first years in school. Late one night, I got up to go to the bathroom and as I tiptoed through the dark hallway past my parents' bedroom door—behind which it was usually silent as the grave—I was horrified to hear my father panting wildly and my mother whimpering softly, sounds I had never heard before, certainly not from my parents. Mother was obviously in danger. There was no doubt she was being hurt, and shouldn't I rush to her defense? But could Father be the culprit?! The shining example, the figure of respect? Unthinkable. I froze. I could never have touched the handle of my parents' bedroom door for fear of witnessing a crime in our apartment. A thunderbolt from my father would certainly lay me low and I would never recover in this lifetime. Did my poor mother cry out? With tears in my eyes, I slunk back to my room, holding my hands over my ears. I would never ever forgive myself for abandoning Mother in her hour of need. In the morning, Father left the apartment earlier than usual. I only caught a quick look at his grumpy expression. He looked right past me. Mother seemed completely unchanged. There wasn't a trace of any nocturnal struggle on her face or hands. But her morning greeting was more curt than usual, and she kept her eyes down as she went about her housework. Now I knew that the three of us—Father, Mother, and me—were truly eternal mourners. Heavy, dark clouds hung over us and I was unavoidably part of this tragedy. But the worst thing was the silence; not a word could be said about it.

The second shock happened soon thereafter. One afternoon, I was stuck in my room working on a big homework assignment. When I finally emerged from my little lair, the apartment was quiet and empty. I was home alone. All the doors were closed. I went into the kitchen to drink a glass of milk and watched through the open window as two boys played down in the courtyard. Then I went to the bathroom to wash my hands and comb my hair. I opened the door and froze with my hand still on the latch. The sight that met my eyes was unthinkable, unimaginable: there before me stood a completely naked woman looking at herself in a big mirror I had never seen in the bathroom before. Father didn't allow any mirrors in the house except for one the size of a plate that he used when he shaved. But the most terrible thing was that the naked woman standing there paralyzed was my mother. I was appalled at her blushing face, contorted with shame and almost unrecognizable. I saw her large breasts with their big, dark nipples, her rounded belly, and below it a black, untamed bush of hair between her wide hips. She remained frozen in the middle of the room, like a living statue. She only hung her head lower than usual. She raised her hands slightly and they twitched in a desperate gesture that replaced the speech against which her mouth was sealed. Only with a scream was I able to free myself from the spell of the situation, a scream that accompanied me as I ran from the bathroom, slamming the door behind me. I rushed into my room and threw myself on the bed, sobbing into the pillows. I would never again look at my mother in the same way. Never, never would she forgive me! My life felt like a gigantic hole into which I had fallen forever, without hope of escape.

I can't remember what happened then. My memory leaves me in the lurch. I do remember, however, that Mother disappeared for the rest of the day, as if whisked away by magic. I can't remember that ever happening before. Father and I ate supper in silence. To my astonishment, he didn't seem to notice Mother's absence. Before retiring early, he addressed a few words of encouragement to his utterly puzzled and bewildered daughter as if throwing me a few crumbs. Late that evening as I lay in my bed, she unexpectedly entered my room, came over, smiled down at me and stroked my forehead.

I was often sick during this time. Mother dragged me from one doctor to another to little effect. My grades got worse, too, which made Father pretty angry. He expected me to always be the best in my class. I was sure that my grades were the only thing about me he was interested in. He seemed not to notice that I was becoming a young woman. Mother reacted to my development with the obvious sympathy she brought to everything that happened in our little family, but it also caused her concern. She seemed to be aging quickly in those years. Only very seldom did I see a fleeting smile on her face.

When I turned thirteen, Father sent me to another school where he thought the teaching was better—meaning stricter— even though I wept at having to leave the girls I had become friends with. But on the very first day in my new school, I discovered a girl I fell instantly in love with—with her adorable face, her gorgeous long hair, her graceful figure! I had it bad. Soon I couldn't think of anything but that girl. I could feel my heart pounding when I asked someone what her name was and they said it was Gloria. I had trouble paying attention in class because I was compulsively looking at her. She sat a few rows ahead of me. I thought I was seeing an angel. Her face was so sweet I thought she must be a creature from another world. She seemed entirely self-sufficient and under the protection of some higher power than the rest of us. She was constantly surrounded by friends—boys and girls—who all seemed to compete for her favor. Not even the teachers could resist her charms.

I didn't know how to approach her. Already shy by nature, I had never felt so uncertain of myself. I couldn't produce even the most common turns of phrase, and my brain immediately rejected anything more creative. I had no defenses against my passion. My days passed in a trance; my thoughts had a single focus.

I suffered unspeakably from my love for Gloria in those weeks, from the unbridgeable gap between impotence and desire.

I tried not to let it show at home. I was sick through and through, but Mother was not able to recognize the illness. Whether I meant to or not, I was confirming Father's opinion that teenage girls were masters of subterfuge.

Deliverance arrived at last. I was traipsing down one of the wide halls at school, absorbed in my thoughts, when someone brushed my right hand for a moment. It felt like an electric jolt. It was Gloria! She said a few words to me as nonchalantly as if we had been friends forever. I had no idea what she'd said and stammered out some idiotic reply. Even so, from that moment on, she and I were no longer strangers passing each other without a word. That's the only thing that mattered, and it transformed my life.

*Father died of a heart attack. He was gone in an instant, with-*out warning. He had always resisted going to the doctor. "No playing for time on the way to God's throne! He'll call me when my hour has arrived," as he put it. And now he was dead before he could receive the last rites. We couldn't even tell whether he was aware of this stigma at the end of his life or not. After supper one night, he suddenly slid sideways out of his chair and landed hard on the floor. He gave Mother and me a parting look of reproach, as if we were responsible for his misfortune, and that was that. We didn't even dare to close his eyelids. That fell to the family doctor when he arrived, a friend of Father's from the church choir. He helped us carry him to my parents' bed. There, he bid him a formal farewell. The doctor's eyes were wet with tears as he said goodbye to us. Only then did Mother and I realize that in our shock and confusion, we ourselves had not yet wept. In the following days, I never saw Mother crying nor any traces that she had; her eyes were not red or swollen. Later she said more to herself than to me, "I've cried so much in my life with him that I finally have no tears left." I missed Father as little as if he had not left us, and it was not long before I began to wonder why that was so and to reproach myself for my indifference and hard-heartedness. In truth, I was so preoccupied with my love for Gloria that there was no room for other feelings.

The funeral mass in our dignified old parish church was a magnificent affair. The entire choir was present, reinforced by

choir members from neighboring churches. The priest dis-
played real emotion in his sermon, but the high point of the
service were the earthshaking chorales of the baroque masters.
A congregation was giving thanks from the bottom of its heart.
Where words failed, the power of music was able to burst the
bounds of the individual. The burial, too, was overwhelming:
we were swept along by the crowd that poured out of the
church and flowed toward the cemetery. At the graveside there
were countless hands to shake—his colleagues from school,
members of the choir, and here and there fleeting apparitions
who introduced themselves as distant relatives. All of this
was in confusing contrast to our withdrawn family life with
Father. At the funeral, Mother and I remained strangers among
strangers.

After my father's death a curious peacefulness settled on
our house, filling every corner. To my astonishment, after three
days Mother told me with unusual decisiveness to take off my
mourning clothes and start enjoying my young life, as she put
it. A little smile flitted across her face as she said it. Almost imperceptibly at first, then more and more noticeably, our days
became lighter. Even the house brightened up. She bought new,
colorful curtains that let in more sunlight. Unexpectedly, Mother
had put aside money in addition to my father's pension, so she
was able to buy us a new set of chairs, new beds, and new kitchen
appliances. When at last our old, discarded furniture stood outside waiting to be carted away, we realized how shabby and
ugly it was and felt ashamed. My opinion was important to her
when we went shopping for new things and she often let me
make the final decision. But she went even further than that:
she insisted that both of us go to an expensive department store
to buy ourselves new clothes and that my wardrobe should

take precedence. She wanted me to look pretty—she even used the word "attractive"—for my girlfriends and for the boys, too. In the dressing room, under the critical gaze of my mother and the saleswoman who waited on us, I had to try on new underwear and a skimpy bikini in front of all those mirrors. I returned home dazed and happy, already wearing a new outfit that showed off my figure. I wasn't used to wearing clothes that showed I had breasts. Before they were always hidden under baggy pullovers. Mother's face seemed to be losing more wrinkles with each passing day and there was a new gleam in her eyes. And although she still spoke very little, we understood each other perfectly with almost no words at all. My allowance was increased and on my next birthday, when I turned fourteen, it was doubled. "You're a young lady now," she said and asked how I wanted to spend this "important birthday." I was a contrary girl and the last thing I wanted was a big party. After endless debate, we finally agreed to invite a small group to our apartment: three girls from my class (one of which was Gloria, of course) and two boys whom I had gotten to know pretty well. This was the core group for my party. When they all stood up to toast me, tears of joy sprang to my eyes. I was happy. I hadn't known I could be so happy. And Gloria sat next to me.

When we were promoted to the next grade, Gloria and I were assigned seats next to each other. At last! We passed little notes back and forth during class, sometimes to ask about an assignment, but usually to make fun of the teacher or one of the boys. In that case, however, we could often communicate just by glancing at each other. With Gloria by my side, I accomplished something Father could never coax me to do: I improved my grades so much (it was almost like child's play), that

I became the best in my class, admired by some and envied by others.

My life would have been happy if something hadn't happened that turned everything on its head. For days, Mother had been acting strange somehow. She hardly spoke to me, her eyes looked like she'd been crying, and she didn't answer my questions. Finally one day when I came home from school, she took me by the hand and sat me down at the table. She looked me in the eye with a troubled expression.

"Christie, I can't stay silent anymore. I got a letter—weeks ago. And now I'm being pressured, pressured by a . . . certain person."

"A certain person" sounded derogatory. I wasn't just surprised by the phrase, I was deeply disturbed. It sounded like she was being threatened. The look on her face scared me.

"Who could be pressuring you, Mother? You've done nothing wrong. If you need help, I'll stand by you. If there's one thing I've learned in school, it's how to get rid of someone who's bothering you."

Mother was breathing heavily.

"It's not as simple as you think, my dear. Things are complicated; the problem goes deeper."

I urged her to tell me more. "What problem? What's complicated? Mother, I think you're seeing ghosts."

"I wish you were right, Christie." She sighed again, as she had a few times already, and I was afraid she was going to start crying.

"Please tell me what's happened! Who is pressuring you?"

She gave me a long, searching look with her big dark eyes, the kind only she could give.

"It's so difficult for me, honey. It's mostly about you. I've been struggling with myself for nights on end. At first, I thought I could keep this letter to myself and the story that goes with it, not bother you with it, leave you in peace, not drag you into it! My God, your own life has just begun and you have a right to live it, to be as untroubled as Gloria and your other friends. I just want you to have a good life—that's all I care about."

My hands rested on hers, my long fingers spread over hers.

"Talk to me! What is this letter?"

She lowered her eyes and pulled a creased piece of paper from her apron pocket. "You must know, honey," she stammered, "that I only wanted to do what was best for you, nothing else."

I sprang to my feet and hugged her even though I was as upset as she was. She pushed the paper across the table to me. As soon as she did it, she began to cry uncontrollably, tears running in little streams down her pale cheeks. She blurted out, "There, read it, read it! But don't be angry! Forgive me . . ." and then she got up and slipped out of the room.

The letter was in pretty bad shape after having been read a hundred times by my mother. The rounded handwriting suggested that a woman had written it. I had to read it over three or four times before its significance had sunk in. My pulse was racing so fast it felt like a fist pounding against my chest, my neck, my forehead. I stumbled into Mother's bedroom. The curtains were drawn and she lay still on her bed, crying. She cried soundlessly, like a hunted animal unable to defend itself.

"Is it true, what this woman—this person—writes? That Father wasn't my father and I'm not your child, but hers? A person I don't even know and have never heard of gave birth to me? And now she says she wants to see me, after all this time. She needs to hold me in her arms or she'll die of grief?! Can this be true?"

Now I couldn't control my tears either. I was distraught and furious. Mother had stopped weeping and she gazed at me in silence with eyes that seemed to contain all the suffering of the world. Her look only fueled my anger.

"So that would make me something like a piece of property, passed at random from hand to hand! And now it's obviously this woman's turn—this person's, if you prefer. Tell her she forgot to ask for my opinion and she can just take her newly acquired maternal love and go back where she came from. Tell her to go to hell! Whatever the two of you worked out—leave me out of it. Leave me alone. This has nothing to do with me! And if you don't agree, then I'll just get out of here and you'll never see me again!"

To give my anger added emphasis, I slammed her bedroom door as hard as I could, ran furiously from the house, abandoned my homework, and without thinking marched the few blocks separating Gloria's house from ours so I could pass a cheerful afternoon and evening with her. I didn't say a word about what had happened. After a brief, chilly telephone conversation with my mother, I stayed overnight as well, the first time I had shared Gloria's big bed with her. I wore one of her nightgowns and we fell asleep holding hands.

That was the night on which, in my uncontrollable anger, I made Gloria's family my own. Gloria would be my sister. Ann, who didn't seem to be carrying around any secrets and could always say clearly exactly what was on her mind in any situation, would be my mother. Albert, a gentleman of the old school, my father. Without ever being aware of it themselves, they became my parents.

Already the next morning, I was filled with remorse. How shamefully I had treated Lena! Without taking the slightest heed of her obvious distress, I had cast her in the role of accomplice to the unknown woman. I admitted to myself that I hadn't treated her fairly, but in my utter confusion I didn't know what to do about it.

Albert had closed his eyes and seemed to be asleep. The two women looked at him. There wasn't a sound in the house although branches were swaying in the wind outside the window. The late afternoon sunshine was mild and the light was beautiful.

He opened his eyes and gave Christie a weary look. "No, Christie, I wasn't sleeping. I was listening carefully, and I am shaken. How could I have been so clueless? Why didn't I recognize how desperate you were?"

She laughed. "You underestimate how clever young women are at concealment. I already told you I was a specialist in subterfuge. And besides, you were my only hope, the father I wished I'd had instead of my biological father or the father who raised me. That's why we're sitting here today and I'm telling you all this!"

"I can remember exactly the first time you were allowed to stay overnight at our house. Ann spoke to your mother on the telephone and she gave you permission to stay. It was a special night indeed for Ann and me. What you couldn't know is that as natural as it was for you to sit down to dinner with us, that's how natural it was for us to welcome you into our house. After we had Gloria, Ann was unable to have another child even though we hoped so much for a little sister or brother for her. We had to submit to unpleasant tests, but unfortunately without success. We had to accept it. From that first night you slept at our house, we felt close to you. Just think of all the concerts and plays you've been to with us in the meantime, the vacations we've spent together, including the one when Gloria had her first attack of depression. At first, we didn't take it very seriously. Remember the mountains in the Valais? All the hikes the three of us went on? They were too strenuous for Ann. I led the way at first, but later I straggled along behind you and watched the wind whip your skirts. Girls didn't wear pants yet in those days."

Wearily he sank back in his chair and looked out the window, lost in thought. Night had fallen in the meantime. Lena's soft voice finally broke the silence. "On the night Christie learned the truth about her birth parents and Gloria's mother called me up, my world collapsed. Now Christie would turn her back and leave me forever. I had lied to her. I kept from her the most important thing a child must know. But had I done something wrong? With my husband's permission, I had taken into my house a tiny little girl whose parents didn't want her. I had taken her as my child, my only treasure. I loved her from the very first moment. She was always the most precious thing I had. And later, when it was just the two of us, it was pure heaven for me. I was so happy, so utterly happy—but only for a short time."

Christie gazed thoughtfully at Lena. She had seldom heard her say so much at a stretch. She slid closer to her on the couch, put her arm around her, and laid her head on Lena's shoulder.

The two women looked at Albert. His head had fallen forward and this time he really had fallen asleep.

The day after that first night at Gloria's, I tried to arrive home as late as possible. Luckily, after class there was a soccer game against girls from another class. After that, I lingered in the ice-cream parlor with some of my friends for a long time. When I finally got home, the apartment was empty. Lena had left a note saying dinner was on the kitchen table. She wanted to leave me alone, she said, since I would surely need some time to myself. Next morning, breakfast was ready on the kitchen table, as always, but Lena still absent. This game couldn't go on forever. I wrote her a note in my energetic handwriting and left it on the table: "Where are you?"

That afternoon we were together again. We gave each other a brief nod as if nothing had happened. But from then on, there was an invisible wall between us. I thought about it day and night: did I really want to see this person who claimed to be my mother, or not? My deep initial reluctance to meet her gave way more and more to curiosity. Who was she? What did she look like? How would she behave toward me? With each passing hour and day, the deeply shaken girl was turning into the offended, indignant female. My self-confidence became boundless.

I held all the trump cards in my hand, not her! She'd better take care how she treated me. I could already picture myself falling on this fishy, guilt-ridden person like a vengeful beast. So one afternoon, I asked Lena, "Where is she?"

As she often did now, she looked at me apprehensively. "She's still hounding me, following me in the street. She won't give up. You can see her if you . . ."

Lena looked out the window down into the street, stretched out her arm, and pointed to a woman standing on the sidewalk across the way looking up toward our apartment—a tall, angular woman, almost gaunt, with a strong, defiant face and a tousled blond mane. She was the complete opposite of Lena in appearance. My first impression was anything but positive. She looked common, low-class, repellent. One thing was certain, even from this distance. There was no doubt I'd been dealt a better hand with Lena. She was standing next to me and I said to her in the sweetest voice I was capable of, "Mother, would you be so kind as to let that woman down there know that I am ready to meet with her? Not here in the apartment, of course not! Maybe in a café or a restaurant, somewhere where I can leave again whenever I want to. At this time tomorrow. For a half hour or so. It shouldn't take longer than that. Those are my conditions. If she doesn't accept them, then we just won't meet. That would be fine with me too. If she ever follows me in the street, she'll get a kick. Also not a problem. I got an A in gym class and I can take care of someone like her."

There was a big strong boy in my class, a year or two older than me, who'd been worshiping me from afar for months. His name was Thomas, and when I asked him the next day if he'd care to come to a café with me that afternoon, he was of course delighted to do so. I told him to sit at another table, at some distance but with a good view of ours. If I gave him a signal, he should come over to our table and then I'd tell him what to do from there. It was a secret mission, I told the eager boy, and I couldn't give him any more information. I gave his chubby cheek a promissory caress and contemplated rewarding him with a kiss after he'd carried out his mission, depending on how it turned out. But by no means more than that; I didn't want to give him too much encouragement.

I dressed simply, as I would have for school: a decent skirt and a bulky pullover, that was it. No makeup.

The person shouldn't get the idea I had made myself up for her. Intentionally, I arrived a quarter hour late for our meeting. She was waiting for me in the restaurant of an out-of-the-way hotel, not exactly a first-class place. At this hour, there was hardly anyone else there. She was sitting at the farthest table in a row and seemed to recognize me immediately as I entered from the street and showed Thomas where to sit. I was surprised to see a man sitting next to her who jumped up as I came in. He was short and fairly stout, without much hair on his head. She came toward me, leaning forward with outstretched arms, and stammered out as if trying to tame her inner agitation, "My dear child, my dear—"

I stopped in my tracks and said brusquely, "There'll be none of that! Either you behave yourself or I'm leaving immediately and you'll never see me again!"

I was very pleased with my performance.

The woman squirmed in nervousness. "Please forgive me. It's the excitement at finally—"

I gave her a severe look, "I advise you to sit back down and avoid making a scene."

She scurried back to her seat in immediate obedience. She seemed fairly desperate. She was about my height and slender. Her face seemed older and more careworn than I had thought from a distance; a woman who had been through a lot. I found her too made-up and her hair was a mess—wild, unruly, and much too long for her age. She probably wanted to pass for a young woman but hadn't had enough money to get her hair done properly. A shifty person, all in all. That was my first impression. But I was sure I was equal to her tricks. "And who is this gentleman with you, if I may ask?"

My voice was sharper and more hostile than I had intended.

"My God, why are you speaking so formally to me?" Her voice was cracking.

"I will address you however I see fit. I think I asked you a question, didn't I?"

"What did you ask again?" Her confusion seemed genuine.

Now the man spoke up for himself in a deep voice and a foreign accent. The name with which he introduced himself sounded foreign too. "I'm just keeping her company. We happened to be passing through town and your mother asked me to come along for moral support this afternoon on this special and very personal occasion. You need to know that your mother is a very emotional and sensitive woman."

"That's exactly right," she agreed. "We have no other connection with each other, not at all. I've had quite enough of men even though I'm still in the prime of life and get a lot of offers. My advice to you, honey, is watch out for men! They're worthless, as I've learned. No sooner do you take up with one and give him your best, he's got his hooks into you and he'll suck you dry like an oyster until there's nothing left. The only exception was your father, but he came from a good family. A real gentleman. At least at first."

In the meantime I had sat down with them and we looked each other over with unconcealed curiosity. A waiter came to take our order and the woman took the initiative with great fanfare.

She suggested one tea or soft drink after another, discussed their merits at length, and then rejected them. She insisted on a certain kind of chocolate cake for me in a way that made it clear she was giving me a special treat. But it turned out the restaurant didn't have that kind and after all the palaver I ordered exactly what I would have in the first place: a glass of water.

This was no day for concessions.

Now the woman began to list all her illnesses for me, interrupted now and then by her escort who would take her hand and nod his agreement and sympathy. But she was on her guard and never took her sharply observant eyes off me for a second. When she saw she was boring me with her detailed medical history, she changed topic and tone of voice in a flash, asking sweetly about me. She wanted to know "absolutely everything" about me, her concern for me on display. She knew so little, after all, which was all the more sad and tragic for her because I was the only child she'd ever had.

I treated her to a few sentences, said that I was doing fine, didn't need anything, and was satisfied with my life.

Suddenly her expression changed. With pursed lips she asked if she could then assume I was financially well-off—a circumstance, she quickly assured me, which she wished me with all her maternal heart. As convoluted as the question was, my answer was a brief yes. This seemed to be highly gratifying to her curiosity. She crowed triumphantly, as if I should be grateful to her, "Then I did the right thing after all!"

Seeing my baffled look, she again switched conversational gears. But first she declared in a subdued voice and with downcast eyes, "It makes me so happy to know you're so well situated. I can tell by looking at you. It's the opposite with me, unfortunately. Appearances are deceiving; I'm literally down to my last meal. I swear it's true. They've even taken away what little savings I had."

Her escort had begun to stroke her hair appeasingly, as if trying to put her wild mane in order. He repeatedly clicked his tongue and shook his head sympathetically. From one moment to the next, the woman again put on a new, more relaxed face and started to talk about the adoption forced upon her by her profession—she was a dancer, a successful ballet dancer as she proudly declared—and her husband, my father. A decision from which she had suffered without end, she assured me, and regretted now more than ever. That was the moment she began to cry and the large tears welling from her eyes had the desired effect on me. I had the impression I was losing control of the conversation.

A glance at my watch showed that we'd been sitting there for almost an hour—my outside limit. I got up.

"I have to go."

She grasped the hand I had offered her and pulled me back onto the seat.

"Only if you promise to see me again. We still have so much to talk about. I'm going away for a few days but I'll be back next week. Then just the two of us can get together—me without my escort and you without your bodyguard. Is it a deal?" She gestured toward Thomas still sitting patiently on his chair and grinning at us.

I said, "Okay," and nothing more. We agreed to meet in the same place. A brief handshake and that was it. She blew me a kiss across the table while her chubby escort stood up and executed a short, slightly ridiculous bow. All the same, I was in quite a turmoil as I left the restaurant, full of nascent emotions—

sympathy for her, sympathy for myself, or both mixed up together? I couldn't tell.

I passed the next few days in a kind of trance. I'd been completely thrown off balance. In school I sat around apathetically.
People asked if I was sick but I didn't want to admit it to myself.
Gloria kept giving me worried looks, took my hand during class
and gave me a reassuring smile.

That was the beginning of the questions that have plagued
me ever since: Who am I? Am I Lena's daughter, Lena who
raised me and surrounded me with love, or am I the daughter of
the woman I met for an hour in a restaurant and who had obviously given me away from pure selfishness, just like that? And
what was worse, was I now inextricably connected to this person through our blood relationship, or with Lena, who was always a true mother to me and in all those years had given me
the warmth and understanding of her profound soul? I had just
turned fifteen; how could I come to terms with the discrepancy?

Lena seemed changed, even though the woman had assured me she would be away for several days and not in the
city. Had she been telling the truth? Was Lena keeping something from me again? Out of pride and timidity I didn't want to
ask her.

As we had agreed, my next meeting with the woman was
just the two of us. We greeted each other without further ado
with a simple handshake, like two opposing parties arranging
a cease-fire. She'd apparently exhausted her previous theatri-
cality. I drank some hot chocolate and ate a bit of ice cream but
turned down the whipped cream. I was already old enough to
start watching my figure, which was also the first thing she remarked about.

"You inherited my figure: tall, slim, sexy, with a pretty face and great hair. We're like two peas in a pod."

I didn't react. To say something nice, I remarked that she'd had her hair done since last time, which led to an extended reply.

"You're right, darling, and high time too, wasn't it? I have to tell you I love my hair so much the only person I trust to do it is a well-known stylist in Paris, a real master, who always smothers me in compliments. I think he'd like to make a conquest of me," here, she giggled, "which has its advantages. He only charges me half his usual outrageous price. I flitted over to Paris for a day or two. It's always such a tremendous adventure: the boulevards, the cafés, the best restaurants in the world, the hotels—pomp and circumstance! You may wonder where I get the money for all that luxury. I wonder myself.

"Well, I've learned how to live modestly. A small hotel, a corner bistro, and a shop next door where you can pick up some pretty things that make you look great. And then there's this or that old friend with a wallet full of money to take me out for a good time—to the opera, to a three-star restaurant. Oh, everything's so marvelous, we should definitely go there together some time. My treat! . . . Uh . . . when I'm flush again. Otherwise, Dutch treat. But mother and daughter would never leave each other in the lurch, right!"

She sighed with happiness.

"You left me in the lurch!" I replied fiercely.

She took her eyes off me and started to powder her nose.

In a loud voice I repeated, "You left me in the lurch!"

She flushed, then resumed her work with the powder puff, carefully checking the results in a fancy little mirror. "I hate having a shiny nose," she remarked casually. "I'm sure you know how it is. It's not so important if you're young, but—"

I rapped my knuckles on the glass tabletop between us and gave the woman a stern look. Another minute passed. She'd stopped powdering her nose. Then she looked at me again and said in a calm, almost relaxed voice, "Honey, you've inherited my stubborn character. Even if you offend people, you'll get your way. Now, what was it you said?"

I was holding my ice-cream spoon and I threw it down on the table. It clattered on the glass. I stood up abruptly and reached for my purse.

Instantly, she hissed, "Okay. You're right. Yes, yes, yes, you're right! But why get so excited? Sit down again. Please. I've already told you how much I regret my decision back then—so much that I'm still suffering from the circumstances that forced me into it. But really, you should have some sympathy for my situation. I was just a few years older than you are now and had a great career as a dancer ahead of me. I was dazzled by the stage, the footlights, the audience, the storms of applause! Just try to imagine it! You should have some understanding for others— especially for your own mother!—and not be so preoccupied with yourself. A little sympathy—"

In that instant, as if of its own volition, my napkin flew across the table and hit her right in the face.

"You're not my mother!"

I don't know whether she heard what I said or not. At any rate, she calmly removed the napkin from her face, then burst out laughing. It didn't seem like she would ever stop. I was so taken aback I couldn't utter a word. Her shrill laughter rattled me completely. She stood up, came around the table, sat down on the bench next to me and put her arm affectionately on my shoulder, and I was unable to defend myself.

"I understand you so well, darling! I understand you with every fiber of my being. That thing with the napkin just now— it was as if you were copying me. Even in little things, you're just like your mother. But now you listen to me. After a long inner struggle, I gave you up for adoption, and I admit that was a huge mistake. What became of my dreams of being a prima ballerina? A year after I gave you away I got a seriously sick: kidney disease! I tell you, the pain was terrible. I writhed in bed and screamed out loud.

"There was nothing I could do: my career was over. After I recovered, I was still able to show off my legs for a few more years in a revue—in the third row of chorus girls on the left. And then . . . oh, I didn't want to have to tell you about this . . . in a cabaret, a sort of striptease, or what they called striptease in those days. I kept my panties on, of course. My figure was still tip-top, especially my bosom, but I definitely wouldn't go any further than that. I would rather have starved. Your father the dandy, always dressed to the nines, had long since taken off, of course. There was nothing more to be gotten out of him. When you were born, he was the first one to suggest giving you up for adoption. He was married and couldn't get divorced because of his family. They were all strict Catholics. An illegitimate child was out of the question. He couldn't inflict that on his parents. He was already angry at me as it was for concealing my pregnancy from him. Forgive me, darling, please forgive me. . . . It's been a hard life, but now I have you back at last."

Her voice had gotten soft. She laid her head on my shoulder

and stroked my hands. I was so numbed and disarmed by her story, which amounted to a confession, that I slid closer to her too and my eyes filled with tears. I don't know how it happened, but somehow I stammered, "Mother, Mother!"

We sat there and hugged each other happily.

When I got home and saw my mother Lena I immediately felt guilty about it. What had I done! But she didn't want to hear anything about it. As I closed the front door behind me, she was right there and gave me a silent embrace. She'd been waiting for me the whole time.

The woman and I had agreed to meet again the next day, but it never happened. She called to say an emergency had come up and she had to cancel our meeting. Her voice on the telephone sounded different, nervous and harried. I definitely wanted to see her again. She now held a magical attraction for me. I had to see her again. I had come to the scary but also inexplicably joyous realization that I was more like this woman than anyone else in the world. I felt exposed. In her emotionality, her flightiness, her keen intelligence, I found a distorted reflection of myself. But I also recognized aspects of her character that frightened me so much I didn't want to think about them. They were too terrifying. Would I end up like her some day? I had begun to love and hate this woman at the same time. And what about her appearance? There was no doubt we looked alike in many ways. I was sure anyone on the street would be able to see I was her daughter, which was never the case with Lena. But at the same time I was ashamed, overcome by a shame I'd never felt before. And so I was hurt, upset, and unhappy not to be able to see her right away again the next day. At the same time, I felt relieved. We had agreed that she would call soon to arrange a new meeting.

But that never happened, and we would never see each other again, I and the woman who was my mother. Never again, except for the incident that played itself out in the street right before my eyes, when I happened to look out the window of our apartment. Yes, it was pure accident that I happened to witness this terrible scene, a scene that pierced my heart. Several classes at school had been canceled so I came home quite a bit earlier than usual. It was still well before noon, and I didn't find Lena in the apartment. I was thirsty and on my way to the kitchen I glanced out the living-room window as usual. I froze in my tracks. On the other side of the street, right where I had first seen the woman standing a few days ago, I saw Lena, the woman, and a strange man. All three were obviously quite agitated. You could easily see it by their gestures and the apparently loud voices they were using. Lena was beside herself with indignation. From that distance, I could see that the other woman was staying in the background. She made only an occasional remark to the other two, then she would take a few steps back, as if she wanted nothing to do with what was going on. The main person in the drama seemed to be the unknown man. He was tall and slim, had a mustache, and wore an expensive suit. He was speaking loudly to Lena and shaking his finger at her.

My first impulse was to rush down to the street to protect her. Then I saw her take a thick envelope out of her purse. She opened it and gave its contents a last glance before handing it over to the man, who snatched it from her. The man took his time counting the bills that it obviously contained. Then he gave a satisfied nod, put the envelope into his jacket pocket, and with a mocking flourish of his hand, bowed deeply to Lena.

She had already turned on her heel and was walking away. The woman trotted after her for a few steps, trying to say something. It looked like she wanted to end the affair on a conciliatory note, but she had no luck. Lena crossed the street with her head held high, looking neither right or left. Only then did I see that our family doctor had been observing it all from a distance. He joined Lena and they walked off past our apartment, side by side.

My head was filled with questions. What kind of deal had Lena struck? Had money been handed over? It seemed obvious it had. Why had Lena paid those two and for what? Was I the merchandise? Was she in league with them? What were they hiding? Why hadn't she confided in me?

And who was the man who had taken the money? Suddenly it hit me: was he my father? Was that my father?!

As I had just a few days ago, I ran headlong out of the apartment and over to Gloria's. As I passed the café on the corner, I saw Lena inside, talking to the doctor who was trying to calm her down. They didn't notice me, thank God! I would not have been able to say a word to them. As I ran down the street I kept thinking, who can I trust? I was running from myself, running in search of a different existence, another life I would discover or invent for myself. I was running to Gloria.

Gloria wasn't home, her mother told me. I was about to go back to our apartment when she asked if I'd like a cup of tea. My distress hadn't escaped her notice. The atmosphere in their house was quiet and soothing and Ann herself exuded a pleasantly calm and relaxed feeling that did me good. Everything she said seemed to me judicious and well-considered. She said that Gloria and her father had gone on an excursion into the countryside. They planned to visit old churches or some monastery;

Ann didn't know the particulars herself. And then she asked me in detail about myself. It was the first time I'd been alone with her and I enjoyed being treated like an adult by this wise and elegant lady. We had a long conversation and the more she took me into her confidence, the more I responded to her. Being with her was extremely soothing after what I had just witnessed. I felt as though all that had been played out on another continent a thousand miles away. Ann must have sensed how happy I was to be with her and how I almost worshipped her. No, she was determined not to let me leave feeling bad.

She suggested we play a game of chess, which my father had taught me. I was no match for Mother Ann, however, and was happy just to be able to put up a little resistance. At last Gloria came bustling in and Ann told her how nice it was to have some time with me and about our interesting conversation and the exciting chess game. It had been a pleasure to get to know me better.

She even said it had given us the chance to become real friends.

Back home I greeted Lena as always and acted as if I had no knowledge of what had happened across the street. For the next few days, I didn't dare ask her what had happened. I didn't want to risk damaging the fragile peace we had managed to establish. I was preoccupied enough with myself in any case. The question that left me no peace was the identity of the man who had taken the envelope with the money. I was convinced it had been about money. But why such a shady handover? There was no end to my questions. Why had the thought occurred to me that the man in the street might be my real father? Was it just my blood speaking? But the way the stranger looked corresponded exactly to the way the woman had described him. I wracked

my brains about how I could find out more about him without upsetting Lena. It was by now clear that she had suffered
enough. But whoever he had been, I never wanted to see him
again. Never. Nor the woman, either. In retrospect, the meeting with her seemed like a nightmare.

For the first time since his death, I longed for my father. Surely
he would have known how to extricate Mother and me from
the maelstrom we were caught in. But he was dead.

There was only one person I could take into my confidence,
and that was my best friend Gloria. After all, we'd never had
any secrets from each other. It happened that her parents had
planned an extended weekend by the sea and I was invited to
come along. Lena had nothing against it. On the contrary, she
agreed immediately since she thought the change would do
me good. They had rented two cozy cabins in the dunes and
Gloria and I had one of them for ourselves. We lay in the warm
sand long past nightfall, looking up at the stars and listening to
the rumble of the surf. I took the opportunity to confide to Gloria the events of the previous days from start to finish, although
it was embarrassing to do so.

For after my confession, I felt quite naked, but I also felt relieved. A weight had fallen from my shoulders. We fell asleep in
each other's arms. The next morning, Gloria promised not to
breathe a word to anyone, she was even ready to take an oath
on it. After thinking it all over, she advised me to put the woman,
the stranger, and the envelope out of my head. The most important thing was not to blame Lena. Just forget it! I gave her a

kiss in thanks and started to cry; she took me in her arms. I would follow all her suggestions except for one: I had to find out the identity of the stranger. Who was he? I had to know.

Life with Lena was not the same as before. Try as we might it was impossible to reestablish our former intimacy. She remained withdrawn and melancholy, as if her will to life had been cracked. The worst thing was that we couldn't talk to each other. The door between us remained locked.

Not long afterward, I was at the doctor's for a routine examination. When I had put my dress back on after the exam and was sitting across from him at his desk, he asked me, "Well, Christie, is there anything else? Anything worrying you?"

He looked steadily at me and his voice had a friendly tone, as if we were equals. I hesitated a moment, then asked him directly, "Was there a lot money in that envelope?"

He answered without hesitation and without apparent surprise, "Yes, it was a pretty large sum, especially for Lena. But it was their price for leaving her—and even more, leaving you—in peace. Anything else?"

I hesitated a long time although it was on the tip of my tongue.

"The man who took the envelope, who was he?" The doctor had stood up and was pacing back and forth. He stopped, tilted his head to the side, and gazed pensively out the window. I looked out too. A lonely tree stood in the courtyard. It wasn't very full and looked like it was trying to decide whether to grow or whither and die.

"Why do you need to know, Christie?"

His voice had taken on a paternal ring. "Is it really that

important to you? What will you get from the answer, what
will it change?"

"Yes," I insisted, "I have to know. If you don't tell me, I'll
have to ask my mother."

He sat down in his chair again with a little groan.

"No, we don't want to trouble Lena with this. Not any more.
She's already gone through enough, don't you think?"

"Then you tell me. Who was he? Maybe he was my father?"

The doctor winced, stood up, and started pacing again. He
was interrupted by his receptionist coming into the room. Un-
willingly, he waved her back out, groaned again, and closed the
door.

"Okay, Christie! I've known you since you were a little girl.
You were always a sweet child . . ."

"And so?"

"Yes. He was your father."

I said, "Thanks," got up, and left his office without saying
goodbye.

The following summer we spent our vacation—Gloria and I—
in the mountains of the Valais. Those were glorious days. It
was the first time her parents had invited me along. Gloria had
been like a sister to me for a long time and we were coming to
resemble each other more and more. We had the same sayings;
our laughs sounded alike. Our bodies were more curvy, too,
but not too much, thank God. We really didn't want to look
like grown-up women yet. But we had definitely developed,
gotten stronger, and we were ready to go on long hikes with
Albert. He was charming to us and we flirted quite shamelessly
with him. He was proud of our company and when we encoun-

tered strangers, he took obvious delight in being in the company of two such pretty young women. Once when we didn't have our bathing suits along, we both jumped naked into an ice-cold mountain lake. Albert was not allowed to look. On the descent, we kidded him and accused him of secretly taking a peek at us. We scaled quite a few peaks, including one ten thousand-footer.

In the evenings we'd lie in our beds, dead tired.

But in was precisely up there in the mountains, the most beautiful place we'd been and in the middle of that carefree vacation, that Gloria for the first time fell into "the black hole," as she called it. I could only look on helplessly as she stared right through me with glazed eyes and didn't answer my questions. At first I didn't understand what was happening. She was clearly in another world, crying to herself. Melancholy had her in its grip. When she was able to talk to me again, we agreed to keep the attack secret from her parents. But Albert soon realized something was wrong. He knew his daughter too well, so well that he noticed the smallest change in her. He and Gloria took the cog railway down into the valley and he had her examined by a doctor, without any success. The doctor was obviously in over his head and said something about temporary adolescent psychosis, perhaps due to interruptions to her menstrual cycle or physical overexertion from mountain climbing. A little rest and a healthy diet would be enough to cure her. So for the last few days, we stayed in our room gazing wistfully out at the mountain peaks that had become our friends. We were bored. As a distraction, Ann introduced us to two French boys who lived nearby. She played bridge every day with their mother. One of them kissed me on the mouth—a fairly sloppy procedure—and the other stroked Gloria's breast, which she later described to me in extensive detail. She fell in love with him and so did I. Gloria was a bit jealous of me. But she seemed to be feeling better, or at any rate, she pulled herself together so as not to worry us anymore. But calamity took its course.

The opinion of the local doctor in Valais proved to be a fundamental misdiagnosis. Gloria's condition continued to worsen, and over the following months she was examined by various specialists. The verdict was depression: serious, hereditary depression. There was a long discussion between Ann and Albert about which side of the family this illness could have come from. Weren't there already signs of it in Albert, his melancholy moods early in the morning and his psychic troughs during vacations— intermittent but unmistakable? It couldn't be denied if they were going to be fair and honest with the poor child in this serious situation. What about his parents and grandparents? Weren't there things that could have suggested a tendency to depression? In Ann's family, on the other hand, there was nothing of the kind. They weren't to blame, although of course there was no question of guilt. Gloria got angry with Ann, whom she blamed for having initiated this "genealogical research." If she didn't stop this "claptrap" immediately, Gloria was going to move in with me and Mother Lena, who always treated her with great sympathy and understanding. Gloria's outburst had its desired effect: they left her alone and didn't burden her with the details of the diagnoses, thank God. Nor did she want to know anything about them.

Then the man they all called Erwin entered Gloria's life.

He was a well-known psychoanalyst whom Albert introduced as his friend. To make it easier for her, Erwin was willing to make an exception and see Gloria at home. And somehow the two of them struck up a relationship. Gloria abandoned her initial reticence and, for a while at least, enjoyed their "conferences" as they called their weekly sessions.

Gloria giggled when she related their conversations and told me how she would test the "nice old gentleman." She confessed her most private sexual fantasies to him, and with the extravagant imagination she had developed in the past few years, she had plenty to offer! The poor psychoanalyst must have blushed scarlet when she gave him her "sugar cubes to suck on," in her words. But she soon lost interest in Erwin and his conferences. She told me in a bored voice that he had nothing more to offer her. She was sick of going over the same things again and again.

We had turned seventeen years old but we were still just two big girls. After the things we had each been through, we had no desire to grow up. Yet we were already more than a head taller than Ann, and even a fraction of an inch taller than Albert. Gloria's illness, her ominously recurring disappearances into no-man's-land, had made her even more beautiful than she already was. At times, her face seemed almost translucent.

When she walked down the street, people would turn and stare. I heard scraps of sentences with words like "angel," "a beauty," and "princess." We laughed about it at home even though I knew that for her, the outside world was rushing past faster and faster. News of her struggle with depression had got around school and she was missing class more and more often because of the attacks. But nobody asked her any stupid questions about it. On the contrary. Everyone respected her and even admired her for it.

Everyone in our class was friendly and affectionate to her. Teachers often gave her a break on grades. But I had to work

twice as hard. Whenever she had to miss class or couldn't follow the instruction because of her condition, I had to go over
what she had missed with her in the evenings or on weekends.
Without planning or even realizing it, I had slipped into the
role of protector and I was happy to accept the job. It made it
easy to suppress my own problems.

Gloria's illness got worse. Albert asked me to accompany him
to a well-known academic psychiatrist. The professor warned
us emphatically that Gloria was at risk of committing suicide. It
should not be taken lightly and it was high time that I, as her
best friend, should be made aware of it. He spoke at length,
as though needing to give us a lecture. He avoided eye contact
with me and kept clearing his throat and stumbling over his
words. Then, after discussing it with Lena and Gloria's parents,
I moved in with her for a while. They cleared out and furnished
a room for me next to hers. There was a connecting door between the rooms that stayed open day and night so we had
continual access to each other. I told her, "If you did something
to harm yourself, I'd kill myself! Or I'd kill you!"

Then we laughed. She swore up and down she would never
leave me. And she kept her promise for a long time. I learned a
great deal about her illness. At first it was Gloria herself who
explained all the details to me (later, she wouldn't talk about it
anymore): she felt submerged in an immense sea of sadness and
had the terrible fear she would never emerge from it again. The
paralysis of all feeling, the freezing up of all emotion. Repeatedly rattling the bars of her cell with no one to hear and no one
to come. The terror of solitude.

And finally, the longing for liberation, for death. Every

fear of the end flown away: death, your guardian angel and redeemer.

One easy step, so near you can touch it. At last, at last to leave everything behind.

But there were other days when she recovered, emerged like a phoenix from the ashes, stepped from the darkness into the light. Where had she been? What beast had had her in its clutches?

Her medications were changed often. They tried one thing and then another, with mixed results.

None of them really helped. Sometimes they gave her some relief, but only for a while. I was in despair and wondered where all this would lead.

Christie laid aside her manuscript and ran her fingers casually through her hair. It had gotten late. There was a thunderstorm outside. The raindrops spattered against the window and then lightning lit up the night. The fire was nearly out on the low hearth. Lena had folded her hands and closed her eyes. Albert rubbed his forehead, stifled a yawn, and smiled a little as if in apology for nodding off. Lena opened her eyes and gave him a smile of encouragement.

"What a moving story you've written for us, Christie! So strange and yet so familiar. You were our greatest help in those days. You were in the trenches. I saw myself banished behind the lines, trying with all my might to maintain contact with Gloria and yet failing. Parents often know so little about their children. They don't learn all there is to know even when a crisis is at hand. But I wasted most of my time blaming God and haggling with him. What had my poor, beloved child done to deserve such suffering? But I want to ask you something: where was Anton in all this? You didn't mention him."

"You're right. I think he was preoccupied with his own development into a man. Did he feel left out? I'm sure he wished for a healthy and happy family, as everyone does. But it was hard to look him in the eye back then. You know what, Albert? I'd rather forget. I really would, if it were possible!"

"After we're gone, Christie. After we're gone there will finally be peace. We have to wait for it."

"My work in Africa demands all my strength. The incredible poverty and the diseases: cholera, typhus, AIDS! It confirms that medicine was the right field for me."

"Yes, I could envy you now. Helping means forgetting."

Christie stood up and stretched.

"I think we should go to bed. That's enough for now. Tomorrow, if you like, I'll read some more. We don't have much time left. I must go back soon."

Lena got up too and stirred the dying fire with a poker.

"To forget . . . in time, to understand. I think that's it."

After breakfast the following morning, Christie took up her narrative again.

Whenever Gloria got better, I slept in my room back home, with Lena. Once when I was home in bed with a fever, Gloria went to the graduation party of an older schoolmate of ours without me. His parents lived in a pretty house with a swimming pool, not far from Gloria's family. In honor of the occasion, the older generation went away and left the whole house to the children— a party with no limits. People flirted, danced, made out, drank, shared hashish and maybe harder drugs. Those who stayed the whole time ended up in the pool, naked or still dressed. I was lying in bed with no idea what was going on at the party, sniffling and coughing, tossing and turning and trying to get some sleep. At midnight or even later, our doorbell rang. Lena came into my room with amazement written all over her face and told me in an agitated voice that it was Gloria. This had never happened before. Gloria was right behind her, came into my room with her coat wrapped around her, teetered sideways a little, and gave a gurgling laugh that turned shrill at the end. I was familiar with this condition. It meant she was wound up and out of control. She plopped onto my bed, sat next to me while water dripped from her tousled hair. She gave me a conspiratorial look. Her speech was slow and deliberate, but occasionally slurred.

"Guess what? I'm drunk! Whoopee! I'm smashed, I'm soooo drunk! I just wanted to let you know!" She lay back and rolled back and forth on the bed. Her coat fell open and I saw she was completely naked underneath.

I gave a little cough. "Hey, Gloria, what kind of getup are you running around in? I can't leave you alone for a second!"

She rolled her eyes and giggled. "How come? Haven't you ever seen a naked woman before?"

"Naked woman? All I see is a naked little girl who escaped from the nursery somehow. And besides, you're going to catch my cold if you get too close."

She flung her coat dramatically into the corner, slipped under the blanket next to me, and snuggled her ice-cold body against mine.

"Nonsense! I can't catch your cold with all this alcohol in my bloodstream. Any child knows that."

"Then you must know it," I countered.

She sat up again, leaned over me, and announced with shining eyes, "You know what happened? I lost my virginity, that's what happened! And it happened without asking you first. I wanted to call you up, but there weren't any cell phones around—we'd thrown them all into the swimming pool."

She paused repeatedly to chuckle and giggle. Still half asleep, I only caught half of what she said.

Finally my curiosity got the better of me. "So tell me how it happened. Did it hurt? Was it great?"

She lay back down next to me and put her still-cold arms around my warm body.

"So: it was a boring party as usual, everybody just standing around like idiots, trying to tell jokes. And we were all dolled up—the girls showing cleavage and some of the guys even wore ties. They really looked stupid! I was looking for a way to make a graceful exit. Then they served lobster—a whole lobster each, very fancy, and good champagne. Freddy, our host, persuaded me to have a taste. I finally gave in."

"You know you're not supposed to drink alcohol! It's completely off-limits! You can't mix it with your medications!"

"Off-limits! You mustn't do that! And you're supposed to be my friend! All these rules all the time . . ."

"Okay, okay. Go on. It's too late anyway—but admit it, you had to barf, right?"

"I did not!" Gloria crowed triumphantly.

"And clearly, you had more than just one swallow."

"It tasted good! Just imagine, I drank a whole bottle!"

"I can believe it, the way you smell." I edged away from her a bit. "And then?"

"When people started to make out, Freddy slobbered all

over my face, then he went down on one knee and declared his love for me. Everybody laughed."

"You were all pretty wasted, right?"

"Oh yeah! Jealous? There was music blasting all over the house. You couldn't even hear yourself talk. The dancing started to be more like a mosh pit. But Freddy was being a real gentleman.

"We wandered around the house and ended up in the swimming pool, the boys in their boxer shorts and the girls in panties and bras. Later, a lot of us took everything off. Freddy took me to his room, showed me his own masterpieces on the walls— gigantic, hectic faces with staring eyes. He asked me if I wanted to do it with him and if I was still a virgin, which I denied, of course. I asked him how he wanted to do it, and he showed me his thing that was suddenly sticking out of his shorts like a carrot: hard and straight. He let me touch it and that was really exciting! So then we just did it, quick as a wink. I screamed some and he pulled his thing back out and squirted the sticky stuff onto my belly.

"You want to smell it? . . . And so, that was about it. I cried a little and he swore he'd love me forever and marry me and then I left. I couldn't find my clothes except for my shoes and coat, and then I came straight here to tell you about it. Pretty nice of me, right? And if you don't believe me, go ahead and have a feel. You do want to be a doctor, don't you?"

"A sociologist," I replied, but she'd already fallen asleep in my arms.

When Gloria woke up, she was feeling sick as a dog. She barfed all over our bathroom. She never said another word about the previous night, as if nothing had happened. She didn't mention Freddy again either; she wasted no time rejecting all his further advances. I sensed she had already resigned from normal life. And I loved her all the more.

Early the next morning, Albert's breathing was labored, as if he couldn't get enough air.

"Outside! I've got to get outside!," he said to himself.

He got up earlier than usual, to the women's surprise. The old man hardly took time to sit down to breakfast. He ate only a little toast, took a few swallows of tea, and then was already storming out the front door. Lena and Christie had to rush to catch up with him. It was a glorious morning. Wearing only a light pullover, Albert greedily drank in the fresh country air. Neither woman wanted to leave him alone with the other.

"I've got to get some exercise before I suffocate," he declared as they walked briskly toward the woods. Albert acted like a young boy. It was as if he was going to start his life anew.

They reached the dark firs and he raised his arm in greeting. "The past, my God, always the past—too much past! We have a right to enjoy today, don't you agree, Christie?"

It was like he was talking to himself, asking himself and answering at the same time. He wasn't even listening to Christie's sympathetic responses. They went right past him. They were taking the same route they had a few days ago. But this time he walked fast and went first if they had to go single file. He ignored a word of caution from Lena, merely laughing. "If I'm too fast for you, don't try to keep up! We'll meet up again on the way back. I won't get lost."

"You will get lost and then we'll have to come looking for you." Lena's voice was full of concern.

He giggled, "This is going to be fun. We're like children again. Who's afraid of the big bad wolf?"

They were already passing through the clearing with the anthill. Albert greeted it like an old friend as they went by.

They reached the green valley. Wasn't this where they had hung up their ghosts? He was bound and determined to go farther than they had a few days ago, whatever the two women thought. No turning back!

He hurried on.

Finally they stopped to rest. Lena got out the sandwiches she had made. Albert ate greedily. Lena had even thought to bring water along. But now the women wouldn't take no for an answer. No more discussion, they had to start back. Albert resisted, but finally gave in.

It had gotten hot. The way back seemed to take twice or three times as long. His steps became shorter. He had to stop often to catch his breath.

But he didn't want to show any weakness, leave himself open to criticism for his impetuous behavior. Had he been reckless? Nonsense!

By the time they got back to the house, his feet were dragging and he was soaked with sweat.

He had just stretched out on the couch in the living room when the telephone rang. It was Ann.

Christie and Lena left the room. Ann's voice sounded constrained.

"I've been here two weeks now and it's been days since we last spoke. You haven't called."

"I'm sorry."

"Why are you sorry? What made you say that?"

"Because I don't know . . ."

"Yes?"

"What to say."

Her voice took on a sharper tone. You could almost see her straightening her back. "Albert, my sister is dying here and you don't know . . ."

"I said I was sorry. I'm very sorry."

"You don't sound well. Are they taking good care of you? You should have stayed at home. Are you sick?"

He gave a little cough. "Not sick, just tired. I'm very tired today."

Albert could hear her heavy breathing.

"I think the end is near. She's having a hard time dying. It's very, very difficult for—"

"I should have come with you, Ann."

"We've just got to accept it now. It's too late to do anything else. We'll see each other soon, at home. Then I can take care of you."

Albert giggled. "There's a giant anthill here. Did I tell you about it yet?"

"I'm expecting the end any time now . . . she lost consciousness hours ago. The doctor says she has a strong heart."

"Like you, Ann."

He heard her start to cry. "Why don't you go home tomorrow? What are you doing there, anyway? Irma's been waiting for days for you to come back, poor thing. She's getting impatient. Tell Christie I expect you at home."

She forced the words out and then started to sob. "I used to be able to count on Christie! What in the world has gotten into her?!"

"You're in my thoughts, my dear. Hugs and kisses—" He heard the click of the receiver.

That evening, Albert went to bed early. He almost snuck up to his room but he again let Lena help him get undressed. He only grunted in response to her good night and immediately fell fast asleep.

It was a leaden sleep that drew him far down into the depths, into caves and grottos and subterranean passages from which he could not find his way back despite the help of Christie and her mother who again supported him on either side. The women gave him reproachful looks. Where had he taken them? What had he gotten them into? He should be ashamed! What was he doing to them when they meant so well? The air was stuffy and getting thin. Was this his thanks for their gift of love? It got darker and darker. He could hardly see his hand in front of his face.

A scream, then another and another. They died away, unanswered. Their echoes, bouncing off the walls, seemed to mock him. At another turning, he had to crawl on his belly to squeeze through and the women had disappeared. Just like that, without a farewell. Had they argued? What did he know? Was the raucous laughter in the distance directed at him? Maybe it was the mother and daughter, glad to have gotten rid of him. In his desperation he knelt down in the wet moss on the forest floor, the forest they had fled before. Was he going in circles? He wept. He cried out a stammered prayer for salvation. This was where they'd hung up their ghosts! This was where he hoped to be liberated. It was here, wasn't it? He was getting everything mixed up. Ann looked at him reproachfully: it's your fault! She was crying. He'd forgotten to take his medications again. It was his fault. You just couldn't count on him, no matter what he promised! Was it Ann's voice that joined the laughter of the other women?

The old man woke up in a sweat. Where was he? He didn't

recognize the room. It took him several moments to get oriented.

Light was falling through the small window. He could hardly move his limbs. Where was his medicine? The narrow door opened without a sound. Lena peeked in with a friendly smile. At least she didn't seem to hold anything against him. Without wasting a word she helped him sit up in bed, took the sweaty pajama top off his hot torso, returned with a soft bath towel and wrapped it around him.

He sank back exhausted, gave her a thankful look, stammered out a few disconnected phrases, still nearer to his ominous dream than to the new day. With her soft hands she touched his trembling lips, arranged his restless arms on his chest, and folded his dancing fingers together. Albert looked intently into her eyes as she put the pills into his mouth without being asked, then gave him a drink of water from a pitcher while supporting his head with her left hand.

It was a while until the medicine took effect. His body was failing to respond, which it had never done before. He'd been fearing this for a long time. Was this the beginning of the end? When he woke up again, Christie was sitting next to him on the bed, looking fine. She spoke to him in a friendly, encouraging way, kissed him on the mouth as only Gloria used to do. She helped him stand up and walk to the bathroom. Then she took him to the living room where he sat down, still feeling punchy and trembling. Yes, they admitted with a laugh, the bathrobe that looked so good on him had been purchased just for his visit.

They spent the day quietly. He let Lena and especially Christie do most of the talking. He listened attentively, returning the loving smiles they gave him. Obviously the ghosts had stayed in the forest, he thought, gone, once and for all!

Before it got dark, he shuffled through the garden and around the house with Lena. Every few steps he would stop and reach for the low-hanging eaves to steady his balance. The old man took only a few bites of the light supper before going to bed. Before he went to sleep, he asked Christie and Lena, "Where am I? I don't know where I am."

"You're with us, with Mother and me," Christie answered.

"Yes, but where are we? I think I need to find Ann."

After a pause, Christie said, "Do you want to go home?"

Lost in thought, he pondered that for a while.

"Home?"

Christie leaned over him and stroked his temples.

"To your house! Home to your place. Would you like to go back?"

"To my place? Yes, to my place . . ."

Then he fell asleep. It was as if he had to catch up on months of sleep in one night. When he finally woke up, he couldn't recall how he'd gotten into bed. It had started to rain. They stayed in the house. When Christie reached for her manuscript again, Albert laid a hand on her arm.

"Christie, I like listening to you read, but I keep coming up against the same wall. I knew she was sick, but I didn't want to believe it. Perhaps I just loved her too much. I wanted her to stay the way I remembered her as a child. But then she became a grown-up woman, a sick woman I was unable to help."

Christie gave him a noncommittal smile and shuffled her papers, eager to resume the story.

Final exams were a torture for Gloria and she just barely passed.

As I said, we were all very devoted to her, including our teachers. But the year before, she had missed half the classes. After graduation, we dived into our university studies. She was going to major in art history and I started out in sociology. I wanted to find out more about humankind, about how much of us is determined by heredity, how much by environment, upbringing, and childhood experiences. For Gloria's sake, I stayed in our town. We both registered at the university. But before we started, I was to spend part of the summer in England. I had won a prize as the best student in our class and was going to spend a few weeks in a small university town on the coast with other young graduates from various countries. They told us we were the elite, and of course we were very proud of ourselves. It was the first time Gloria and I had been apart. I promptly fell head over heels in love. My life up to then—even Gloria—was suddenly all very far away. I felt terribly guilty, but at the same time, felt I was starting life anew. The program only required us to hear a few introductory lectures on the European Union, the United Nations, UNESCO, aid for the Third World. The point of the whole thing was probably to encourage us to study international relations.

The boy was already twenty, an Irish boy with curly red hair like I'd never seen—much less touched—before. He had freckles across his nose and the most enchanting smile in the world. That smile just knocked me out. He wasn't too shy, but he wasn't a big Casanova either. He was just sweet. His father had a castle in Ireland that had belonged to the family for centuries, with lots of horses. But best of all were the flower beds, flowering shrubs, and the huge old trees. They were tended by almost a dozen gardeners even though the family had almost no money left, he said. That's why he had to become a cabinet secretary or something, and then he smiled at me, burst out laughing, and I believed every word he said.

Whether coincidentally or fatefully, his name was Fred. Of course, I dubbed him Freddy the Second, which drove him crazy until I explained why. It only took us a few days to become a couple. When we'd had enough of holding hands and kissing, we slept with each other in my room, which was of course against all the rules. We got my roommate to move out for a night. Fred said his mother had brought him up not to know anything about girls. Then he was sent to a boarding school with not a girl in sight—actually, he should have turned out gay. But despite this sad past, he proved to be quite good in bed. We bid each other a very tearful farewell. With his father's permission, he invited me to visit him in Ireland. He would be able to bring his mother around as well in the meantime.

Now Gloria no longer had a head start on me. When I spilled out my story about Freddy the Second her reaction was quite restrained, even cool. "Okay, so you've fallen in love. So what?" was the extent of her reaction.

Time flew by. On my nineteenth birthday, I was allowed to go to Venice with Gloria and her parents. The city was radiant in the autumn light and completely beautiful. But the trip turned into a fiasco. Gloria was suddenly ensnared in her depression, clammed up and lay on her bed with glassy eyes. The rest of us slunk through the narrow streets, stared at San Marco and the Doge's Palace, but all that beauty and grandeur meant nothing to us. The only thing I can recall is that we stayed in a huge old palace that had been remodeled into a hotel and smelled strongly of dust and mothballs. In the evenings, a couple of drunk Americans sat in the bar and whistled at us. We were glad to return home.

During Christmas vacation, I was scheduled to visit Fred in Ireland. I was so excited! Gloria asked if she could come along and of course I agreed. I wanted her to meet my darling. But everything turned out different than I expected. Fred seemed different. He was polite but quite reserved. I couldn't tell whether it was out of regard for his parents, who made us feel extremely welcome, or for some other reason. The castle, its park, and the whole landscape were wonderful but Fred and I just didn't seem able to reestablish our earlier spontaneity. We only slept once or twice with each other, and not very successfully. Gloria seemed changed as well. She was almost forward with Fred's parents and flirted with him the whole time. She dominated the conversation as if she wanted to steal my show. We'd become rivals.

I was going crazy. On our last night there, she slipped into my room with tears in her eyes and all trembly, smothered me with kisses, and kept begging me to forgive her. She admitted she was jealous. It had overcome her like an infection and she couldn't help herself. We lay in each others' arms and she kept reaching for me as if to establish ownership. In that night, it became clear that I would have to make a difficult decision.

Next day at the Dublin airport, Fred surprised me with a passionate goodbye kiss completely at odds with his behavior during our visit. Back home, it was no longer in doubt that I would have to choose between Gloria and Fred. One or the other, I couldn't keep them both. After a long struggle, I realized Fred would survive very well without me, but Gloria wouldn't. Still, I loved him.

One or two months later, he and I met again in London. Fred had rented a large room with a garden. The city was wrapped in such thick fog that I basically saw nothing except

Fred and his bed, where we spent most of our time. He was twenty-one by then and wanted to prove how much whiskey a real Irishman could hold and how much love he could give. We egged each other on. I hadn't realized what passion the human body was capable of. Fred grew more and more radiant. In his own eyes, he had passed the test. He saw clearly into the future and thought I was completely devoted to him. I was certainly obedient, he was right about that: I responded to the slightest pressure from his thighs like a well-trained mare. We would make a splendid couple. After graduating from university we would get married, he explained, and then have lots of children. He was completely convinced of his plan. His parents' blessing was a foregone conclusion. My future in Ireland seemed assured.

By contrast, however, the closer our bodies became, the less I loved him. I felt emptier with each passing day. Finally, there was nothing left but sadness. It was like a farewell from love, with Gloria visible in the background.

After a few years at university I changed majors. Sociology didn't offer what I was looking for. I thought of myself as a tangled skein of yarn and sociology had nothing but empty phrases instead of solutions. So I switched to medicine and found what I sought. I was soon completely engrossed in my studies. Again I was seized by the ambition to be the best. Gloria seldom appeared on campus, even when she was feeling well.

She had met a well-known painter who got her into the

academy of arts. Her passion for painting was nothing new and now she could indulge it fully. She proved to have an unfettered imagination. I felt miserable after breaking up with Fred, but Gloria made up for the loss a hundredfold. At that time, she was the most enchanting friend imaginable. She blinded me with her triumphant, radiant beauty, showered me with presents, hugged me at every opportunity. She was rewarding me. It was an honor to be her friend.

But the price was my Irish redhead.

Then came the big crash, what you'd have to call her first really serious breakdown. Gloria was admitted to a hospital . . . sanatorium . . . clinic . . . whatever you want to call that place, that scourge of God. It was the step we had always feared so much. In her manic state, she couldn't be treated as an outpatient anymore because the risk was too great. Something could happen to her any time, any day. The doctors were unanimous that she had to be protected from herself. In his zeal one young psychiatrist with darting eyes and bad posture even made the outrageous assertion that the world needed to be protected from Gloria. He had the gall to say that to my face, and I flipped out and started screaming that he'd better watch what he said or he'd need protection from me, not the world from Gloria.

Those were bad days. I couldn't look Ann or Albert in the eye. After one attack, an attempted escape, the nurses restrained Gloria in her bed and shot her up with tranquilizers. We weren't allowed to see her. It went on for days while time stood still and nothing moved. The doctors had taken the decision making out of our hands. It's worse than death, I thought.

. . .

Albert had been sitting quietly in his armchair, listening with his eyes half closed. Now he jumped up, knocking over a little table with books and magazines that fell clattering to the floor.

"No, no, that's a lie!" he yelled, his voice cracking. "It was never like that! Nobody ever tied her down. I wouldn't leave the hospital until the doctors promised me that. If they hadn't, I would have stayed beside her day and night, holding her hand. I would have slept by her side."

He trotted up and down the room in agitation, holding his trembling hands clasped as if in prayer. Lena bent down to pick up the books and magazines while Christie stared impassively out at the sunny day. As Albert sank exhausted into his chair, he said quietly, as if to himself, "Forgive me, please forgive . . ."

Christie swung around to him and tried to smile. "No, no," she choked out, "it's me who should apologize."

Lena straightened up, half raised her right hand, and exclaimed in a dark, emotional voice that caught the other two unawares, "What are you talking about?! Have you both lost your mind? No one needs to apologize, neither one of you! It was beyond your control."

Albert put his hands up to his temples and whispered, "She was my child . . ."

"I summoned the ghosts," Christie stammered. "It's what you wanted, Lena."

"It was years ago, but time doesn't exist. What's here is here, and what's not here is not here." A big smile lit up his face as if he'd found the key to his peace of mind.

"She's here; she's with us, and that is happiness."

The room had gotten cool. Lena closed the windows. She refilled their teacups. Her expression had become placid again. She went over to her daughter and stroked her hair. "You're telling it the way it was. Give yourself peace as well. You'll soon be at the end of your story, Christie."

"Yes, I have to finish it tomorrow. Then I must leave you."

*They had already assembled early in the morning to take ad-*vantage of their last day. Albert was unshaven and looked quite dashing. Half pirate, half philosopher was Lena's assessment. But she liked him that way.

Christie had tried several times to explain to him that their time was short. She had to leave tomorrow. She had a plane reservation and she was expected in Africa. And besides, didn't he have to get back to town? Ann could be back home any day, any hour.

But the old man seemed not to understand. His thoughts were elsewhere and he had lost some control over his body, his limbs. Lena spoke to him with patient insistence until he smiled at her and nodded, as if he agreed to everything.

Christie took up her story again.

Gloria stayed in the clinic for a long time, much longer than we'd expected. Days turned into weeks and weeks into months. We were only allowed occasional visits, and were happy when the weather permitted us to leave the bleak visitors' lounge and take her out into the sparse garden with its high walls. The sight of other patients—distraught, with staring eyes, being ungently herded down the long corridors by male nurses—wasn't exactly edifying. On the contrary.

Gloria was pale. The light she used to radiate seemed extinguished. It was as if you could see right through her.

When they finally released her, they wouldn't say she was cured, only improved and in remission. The impression you got was that she had lost her vital power. The doctors treating her were distanced, almost uncaring, as if to emphasize their disengagement from the problems of their patients. Their words of farewell were curiously cool and kept us at arm's length. Yes, we could take her home if we insisted, but at our own risk. The young psychiatrist I had tangled with seemed completely focused on acting professional. You could sense his ambition to get to the top on the fast track. His patients were the more or less welcome sacrifices he had to make. It was easy to see he didn't want to let Gloria slip from his grasp. He opposed releasing her to the very end and only gave in when the chief of psychiatry said she could come home, to our great relief. How I hated that young psychiatrist. I lay awake at night and shuddered to think how easy it would be to murder him. I could picture my hands closing around his skinny neck, cutting off his air for good.

When Ann, Albert, and I got Gloria home—back to the house where she had grown up, she ran right up to her room without taking off her coat and sat down on her girlhood bed, then looked around with a frown.

"I don't want to live here. I'm not a child anymore. Can't you rent an apartment for the two of us? Soon?" She gave me a shy smile, as if she felt guilty.

Why should she feel guilty? Why indeed. I thought about it for a long time, racking my brain. I came to a conclusion that made me very, very sad: she was ashamed, ashamed to be sick. And she got angry when she caused us worry or trouble. But she said repeatedly: I'm ashamed of myself.

In just a few weeks we moved in together. The apartment we were looking for couldn't be too big or too beautiful to satisfy Albert, but Ann urged frugality. We were barely twenty years old. There was almost an argument about it. Finally, a nod from Gloria was all it took (she was still the princess) and we moved into a roomy place with a lot of natural light and a little terrace garden with a broad view out over the city. She regained her strength. But the weariness she had brought home from the clinic remained, due surely to the strong medications she had to continue taking. It was a life in slow motion that had enveloped her. For me it was something new and unfamiliar. Getting up in the morning and using the bathroom used to take only a few minutes. Now it often cost her an hour or more. She tried to collect her thoughts over breakfast. What was scheduled for today? Was it worth the effort? Shouldn't she cancel things?

Why even try? Sometimes three or four times in succession she would ask after people we had already talked about at length the day before. Was it memory loss or indifference?

She didn't know the answer herself. To escape her confusion, she would write her appointments for the next few days on little slips of paper. She often added amusing graffiti and fantastic arabesques. Tanguy had become her favorite painter. Prints of his paintings decorated the walls of our apartment, whether I wanted to look at them or not—disfigured figures, the often cute little creatures tumbling over each other, playing with each other, stretching out, exposing themselves.

She went to the Academy of Arts only sporadically, just to visit. She took her sketchbook along, listened to the professor attentively, dreamily, amiably, but her thoughts were elsewhere.

The results in her sketchbook were meager. After hours of work there might be only a few lines, some circles, but they could be delightful. Later she started drawing caves, more and more caves. Sometimes there were nests that lured the beholder into their depths—caves and nests to hide in, to disappear into. Then she was seized by passion. The pages on which she worked got larger and larger, her line darker and more confident. If she used color at all, it was very sparingly applied. Now her work seemed inspired by protest and revolt.

Some of her drawings, executed with an easy hand, were greatly admired. They put up an exhibit of them in the foyer of the academy for several days and it was abuzz with the voices of faculty and students: "Where does she get her ideas?" "She's never here, is she?" "Has she been sleeping with Picasso?" "She's amazing, this woman. If she keeps it up, the academy is going to have a genius on its hands!"

Gloria made her way through this chorus like she was walking through a gentle summer shower. She flashed a shy smile now and then, but didn't seem to be listening. When people spoke to her in the halls, in class, or in the cafeteria, she dropped her eyes and said only one word, "Thanks."

By evening, she had forgotten all about it. I think it just didn't interest her. All those people and what she called their "chatter" were far from her thoughts. She herself was the only one who counted.

One day someone I didn't recognize showed up at the academy. At first I only saw him from the back as I passed behind him. I watched him lean in close to examine her large-format drawings, even remove his glasses and almost touch the paper with his nose. Then he turned around abruptly, as if he'd been waiting for me.

"I'm Dr. Kornbluhm." My archenemy! Why was he introducing himself when we knew each other already from the psychiatric hospital?

"You're here?" I couldn't think of anything else to say.

"Yes, if you'll allow me—you as her alter ego."

"That's not an answer, Doctor. We're not in your hospital anymore."

"No, of course not. I know you hate my guts. That goes with the territory. Happens all the time. No problem."

He had his glasses in his hand and was giving them a thorough polishing with his handkerchief. "But sorry I can't agree with you. Once a patient, always a patient."

"You know what? It would give me great happiness to murder you."

"Pleasure, dear young lady! Pleasure, not happiness. Why not do it then? This is your chance. But it wouldn't solve your problem, only deprive your friend of help. So I advise against it. And why are you so critical of me? Shouldn't the two of us work together?"

Aha, I thought, so now I'm his accomplice.

As he spoke the last sentence, he blushed. I was horrified by the sudden thought that he could have a crush on me. He was devouring me with his eyes.

"And how do you like Gloria's pictures, Doctor? Are you surprised?"

"On the contrary! They're just what I expected. Brilliant, but consistent with her illness. They're images of sickness. And since we can't understand them, can't discover their source, we're fascinated and fall prey to their riddles without realizing it."

I was speechless. For a few seconds I stared at him standing there before me like an overgrown schoolboy, then I slowly turned and left without another word.

With only a few exceptions, I had to go everywhere with her. She was incapable of crossing the street by herself, she declared. It seemed impossible to her. Once I saw her standing alone at a corner. She was just standing there, patiently waiting. The light changed from red to green and back to red and back to green again. Finally she found the courage to ask a man standing next to her to help her cross the street, like a little child.

I had too little time for my studies. I still wonder how I ever passed my intermediate exams. I really just muddled through them. I literally learned in my sleep, with the books under my pillow. Since I had the reputation of being a good, hardworking student, my evaluations were always good. Gloria and I, we were the quadruped: two healthy legs and two sick ones. The well half had to be there for the sick half, when Gloria needed a piggyback ride. When I actually gave her one because she looked too tired or too slow, we'd laugh out loud about it. She was really not a heavy load anymore. During her months in the sanatorium, she'd swallowed almost nothing except medications. When I hugged her it felt like I was holding nothing much more than skin and bones in my arms. But when she was naked in the bathtub, you could see that she was still a very beautiful young woman who could arouse admiration and even wonder. A seductively beautiful woman. But her former radiance was gone. In its place, she was wrapped in a fluid veil of otherworldliness. She moved as if she was the only person in the world, even though she always wanted me nearby and lay pressed close to me at night.

She was moody with her parents, irritated by their loving concern. Gloria withdrew from Ann and Albert more and more, especially from Ann, who often lost her head and smothered her daughter in too much sympathy in a desperate attempt to do the right thing. Sympathy was the last thing she needed, especially from her parents. One time, when she'd left the two of them standing at her front door not knowing what to do, she said, "It's all their fault. I hate them for having me.

"No, it's worse than that, I don't even hate them. Shouldn't we move somewhere else where no one can find us? To the mountains or to the shore?"

Although I was always on watch, always afraid of a new crisis, we tried to live a normal life. I did, at any rate. When she couldn't summon the courage to leave her bed and lay there staring intently at the ceiling for days on end, I would break out in a cold sweat. Was it starting again? Would I have to call upon the monsters in lab coats again, the man with the thick glasses? Would I have to take her back to that prison when she'd already brought herself so low? Once I found her standing at the edge of our terrace, leaning much too far out over the railing. I screamed, then clapped my hand over my mouth as she turned around dreamily.

"What are you afraid of?"

Then she grinned as if she'd told a good joke and like a coward, I joined in her giggling and cawing.

For weeks at a time she wouldn't leave the apartment, wouldn't take phone calls, wouldn't answer any of my questions. I didn't dare leave the house for more than a few minutes, and only for the most essential purchases. Panting, perspiring, I would rush back to the apartment. I called Albert. I needed his advice and help. He came alone although Ann had insisted on coming too.

He told me they'd had a terrible argument about it at home. He only saw Gloria for a few minutes. To make things as pretty as possible for you, I had her lie on the chaise when her father arrived, she was lost in her thoughts and fears and staring up at the sky where some clouds were passing. She seemed not to see him. Albert and I sat despairingly on the steps from the terrace up to the apartment door and he said, "One more day, Christie! One more day, please. Can you hold out? If we hire a nurse, she'll know how bad it's gotten again. Please, Christie, just one more day."

I knew he meant tomorrow and tomorrow and tomorrow. But he could also see that my whole body was trembling. And then a miracle happened. The next day, Gloria got up, rubbed her eyes, did some calisthenics on the terrace, ate a big bowl of granola, and asked, "Did something happen?"

And then we laughed. Later she hugged me, kissed me on the mouth, and whispered into my ear like a lover, "You're my angel. Somebody pulled me out and I think it was you, Christie. Yes, I'm sure it was you."

The days and days of desperation were gone with the wind. The thought that went through my head was, No, no, she's the angel. Hasn't she already set off for heaven?

One day, Gloria brought her old boyfriend home, Freddy the First, who was responsible for the loss of her virginity. He seemed embarrassed, shambled around the apartment like an old pedant inspecting the furniture, expatiating on its design, lecturing us at length on new avant-garde ideas from Italy, lingered provocatively beside our queen-sized bed and asked ambiguously, "What's going on here?"

Freddy had followed in his father's footsteps and gone into the fashion business. He was decked out in elegant designer clothes and claimed he was already a junior partner in the family firm. A few months ago he had gotten married to the daughter of a rich industrialist. Too bad we hadn't come to his spectacular wedding! We hadn't even answered the invitation. And they had wanted Gloria, good old Gloria, as the maid of honor.

It turned into a boozy evening. One after the other we drank champagne, whiskey, beer, and vodka and spooned foie gras straight out of our last remaining tins. Gloria brushed away my warnings dismissively, ignored her medications. Freddy had become a great ballroom dancer. Rumba, samba, and tango were his specialties. Gloria and I took turns dancing with him and he revealed his inner Casanova. He pressed us against him one after the other, claiming it was part of the dance. As a bonus, he whispered sweet nothings into our ears, French-kissed whichever one of us he was dancing with, and exclaimed excitedly, "A night of love with two women! It's what I've always dreamed of!"

Gloria was sitting on his lap and unbuttoning his shirt when she suggested, in a voice that had become somewhat slurred, that we invite Freddy's wife over too.

"What do you mean, two women? Three are much better for a pasha like you! And anyway, I'd like to meet your sweetie."

As soon as Gloria mentioned his wife, Freddy hesitated, put on a serious face as if he was at a funeral, and babbled, "We pledged never-ending loyalty to each other! I'm serious! Till death do us part." His eyes teared up. "I'm a decent guy!"

Gloria tickled his bare chest to mollify him. She'd already removed his shirt and thrown it onto the floor.

"Then you're in good company here! But don't forget: you

were the first one to do it with me and that gives me certain
rights, especially if I was almost your maid of honor! Maid
rhymes with laid!"

Not long afterwards, I could hear the squeaking and groan-
ing through the wide-open door to our bedroom. I wanted to
get away and not listen. I went over and turned up the music. I
started to move, repeating our dance steps solo on the bare
floor. I was fairly tipsy. I remember that in the middle of the
night, we were all sitting on our "marriage bed" drinking the
last bottle of champagne. Just when Freddy was getting really
comfortable and rolled over on his side to go to sleep, Gloria
summarily tossed him out of the apartment and we slept off
our hangovers. Gloria's affair—or rather, her escapade—with
Freddy lasted a few weeks and then ended as abruptly as it began. We set off for the Caribbean.

"I remember visiting you before you left," Albert piped up. "After weeks of silence, you invited us to dinner. Ann didn't want
to come. She was enormously bitter. We argued and yelled at
each other. She felt excluded. She wept and claimed I was stabbing her in the back. I finally persuaded her to come along."

"We had spent hours shopping for the best ingredients and
doing the cooking. We opened the best wines we had and Gloria
took only little sips. We lit candles all over the apartment."

"Yes," Albert said, "it was a celebration! A great evening! It
was a reunion and a farewell at the same time. I was deeply
moved and very happy. I think I've never been that happy again.
I told myself that all our worries were over. On this big trip,
Gloria would begin a new life. We looked to the future with

hope and I was unwilling to see or hear anything to the contrary. Back home, I put my hands over my ears and refused to listen to Ann's prophecies of doom."

*We flew to Cuba, mainly for the music, but we were also ex-*cited about Castro and Che's revolution. When we arrived in our hotel, a cheap flophouse, I was terrified to discover that we were on a narrow tightrope again: her eyes had suddenly gone glassy. She couldn't recall the few phrases of Spanish she had taken so much trouble to learn, and I had to lead her like a child through the hideous lobby of our hotel. The first few days, she'd only go out into the streets for a few minutes, ate hardly anything, and slept day and night. I was starting to look for return flights. The hotel owner had put a little cage with a tiny bird in our room, and its cheerful chirping filled the air. Gloria and I stood on the balcony with our arms around each other and avidly took in this foreign city, this new world. The little bird moved her to tears. We could look into open windows where naked children, women in colorful underwear, and men in dirty pajamas were running around. All around us the buzz of voices—bright, dark, loud, and tender—cats meowing, dogs yapping and howling, horses whinnying, music in all keys and rhythms, and the constant background noise of never-ending traffic, the honking of ancient cars of all makes, sputtering motorbikes, distant ships' horns from the harbor, church bells, and the roar of landing airplanes sounding like they must be heading right for our roof.

"Should we stay here, or hadn't we better to go back?" I cautiously inquired.

"Back? Back? No! Just give me a little time," Gloria whispered.

Out of gratitude we set the bird free and gave the owner a kiss and a dollar bill in return. We crisscrossed the island in a battered Ford, ate grilled fish and drank cheap country wine in little villages. Then we lay naked on the endless sandy beaches and smoked the oversized cigars someone had given us as a present. I recall getting sick from them. We kept watch for sharks in the water, but we were obviously not worth their effort. Once we discovered a baby shark right in front of us in the water—he looked enormous—and we were so afraid of one another that none of us dared to move. Finally he turned and swam away with great dignity and without a backward glance.

In a week we were already almost as brown as the Cubans. Only our blond hair, bleached in the Cuban sun, betrayed us as foreigners. Men cast burning glances in our direction but treated us with respect and unforced courtesy. It was wonderful! Why couldn't it be like this everywhere? Gloria was delighted. The people we encountered were poor but very dignified. We felt better with each passing day.

Gloria still wept a lot, but she smiled at the same time. She said I shouldn't worry about her tears. I think she was leading a double life in those days, deeply melancholy and yet full of joy.

Only once she said, almost casually, "It's hard to keep going. I feel like a trapeze artist. All that's missing is a sequined costume. I'm flying through the air and I'm terrified of falling."

Then one morning, while she was still asleep, we got a telegram from the clinic where she'd been locked up just a few months ago: "Patient is due for routine examination. Have

learned she is in Cuba with companion. Consider trip irresponsible given patient's unstable condition and advise immediate
return to avoid risks."

Following the signatures there was a postscript: "See you
soon. Love, Ann."

As gently as possible, I attempted to let Gloria know what
was in the telegram. As always when there was something she
didn't want to hear, she didn't react. In the evening I threw the
telegram into the wastebasket.

At a street festival we got to know several families—children
and grown-ups all together. They invited us to magnificent
feasts in tiny apartments overflowing with people. They were
simple fishermen and we asked them where we could learn
how to scuba dive. An old man had an idea.

He said we should go to the nearby Cayman Islands. They
had the best diving locations in the Caribbean and good teachers. There was a flight every week that we wouldn't have any
trouble getting on as tourists. But if we wanted, he could also
take us in his boat the next time he went there. He didn't say
what took him to the Caymans.

Before dawn a few days later, wearing our backpacks, we
found ourselves boarding his tiny fishing boat in an out-of-the-
way harbor. He was going to take us the hundred miles across
open water, and we were feeling a little queasy about it.

The fisherman gave us a confident smile and said he had
often undertaken this trip. It had gone well every time. So we
shoved off, joined at the last second by a small boy who skill-
fully untied the painter and made a daring leap into the wobbly
boat.

In fact, the trip was much less dangerous than we had feared.
For most of the way, the sea was smooth as glass and soon the

sun was beating down on us. By noon, we landed in a little bay on Cayman Brac and said goodbye to each other. After a long walk we reached a village where we rented a room in a guesthouse and went to sleep, dog-tired.

The following day we took a boat to the next island, the isolated Little Cayman, where we learned how to dive. After only a week of lessons, we proudly had our certificates in hand. We took long trips around the island in the boat of the bearded diving instructor, stopping from time to time to dive. I saw Gloria kiss him. Then she slept with him in our little bungalow by the water. He was an Australian who had come here seeking solitude. For me, there was no doubt that this touchingly simple man had fallen head over heels for Gloria. He taught us how to overcome our fear of the depths, to dive headfirst into the deep with the heavy oxygen tank, how to clear our ears to avoid the pains of changing pressure, how to use the computer and give the correct hand signals. I especially recall the one with the hand palm-down and drawn flat across your throat. It means "I'm not getting any air!" Then there was the vital decompression when ascending from depths of thirty or forty meters. We were astonished at the world of endless diversity and the iridescent colors of the fish: angelfish, butterfly fish, the snapper family, the perch, not to mention the ugly, frightening barracuda and the long, skinny needlefish. A dreamworld!

Gloria wrote about her underwater experiences on scraps and sheets of paper that fluttered through our bungalow. Later, she used this kind of diary to write down things that moved her. She never looked again at what she'd written and left her papers lying all over the place. I carefully collected them and put them into a box.

On one of them, she wrote, "It began with the fish, at least

I think so. The big dark brown thing came swimming out of a hole they call a tunnel and looked at me with a touch of superciliousness in his small, sorrowful eyes. He had every right to. He lives here, after all, and I'm nothing but a temporary intruder at best, someone to put up with. I serve no purpose and in the end am just disturbing his peace. He seemed almost as long as I am tall but I'm probably exaggerating terribly because everything looks much bigger underwater. So let's say he was as long as my legs at most. He was beautifully slim and that gave him a special gracefulness. We swam alongside each other for a while and I was delighted that the fish was favoring me. Actually, I was a little behind him, he allowing me to be his entourage for a limited time. I admired the heavy stripes on his sides and his elegant movements.

"I raised my hand as if to say, All the best, my friend! Stay well! Above all: stay clear of humans. Don't let them catch you. I also thought, Why can't I be a fish? How much happier I would be. I would take this fish who's allowing me to follow him as my husband—I was sure he was a male—and I'd be faithful to him and bear him many, many tiny baby fish. Life beneath the surface seems to me lighter, simpler, without the fearful burdens people have to shoulder. Won't you accept me into your secret kingdom? I wish I could dive and dive, farther and farther into the darkness of the sea, deeper and deeper until it gets still and stiller."

The best day was when a giant stingray sailed past a few meters above us like a majestic UFO, with huge outspread wings almost near enough to touch. We swam along in his shadow for a while. Hours after the encounter, already back in the boat, Gloria could still hardly contain her excitement. She hugged George and me again and again. That was the day I thought we had finally left all our troubles behind, once and for all.

Back home, we paid dearly for our wonderful trip. Gloria's condition started to get worse the day we returned, so much so that after many consults, tears, and desperation there was nothing for it: we had to admit her to a clinic again. Ann, the strongest of us, had insisted on it. Albert was speechless, his face a mask of stone. Even I was unable to get Gloria to talk to me. She was completely passive and apathetic. Ah, if only we had remained on that remote island with George! Once, Gloria gave me a meaningful look and drew her hand slowly across her throat. It was our secret sign. Emergency! Emergency!

On the day they came to pick her up from our apartment, I couldn't go another step. My feet let me down.

Gloria looked at me again and, to my horror, again drew her hand across her throat. They strapped her to a stretcher and carried her out. I thought, Is this farewell forever? But thinking about Gloria was what kept me alive.

It was forever until we got her back. When we did, we drove up to the Valais, Gloria, Ann, Albert, and I. We had a doctor came with us, a wise, experienced man who had long conversations with her every day—Erwin had turned up again, undaunted. Apparently nothing could upset him. But he had no luck with Gloria. She remained unapproachable, inwardly lifeless; a wan smile, a few words, that was all. When Erwin and her parents finally left, she and I had two or three peaceable weeks by ourselves. She came along on our old trails up into the mountains—for part of the way, at least. We made the acquaintance of the headstrong mountain goats with their comical faces. They bounded along behind us, bleating and apparently laughing at us. Gloria bleated back loudly. Then it was high time for me to get back to the university, and we left.

"I never want to go back to that clinic," she told me on the trip home. "If it ever gets to that point again, tell me beforehand, Christie. Please, Christie, do that for me. If I don't hear you, scream it in my ear, scream until I nod my head. Promise me! It was even worse this time. I'd rather die than go through that again!"

George was waiting for us at home, a surprise for Gloria.

"I couldn't go on without you, Gloria," he said. "Wouldn't you like to go on a trip together? I want to show you the desert. The desert and the sea are the best things we have. But the desert is even quieter than the ocean."

I think he had come to save her. Australia was too far, so they flew to Morocco, south of the Atlas Mountains. They traveled for several days with Mohammed, a tall, gorgeous Tuareg tribesman in long, bright blue robes. Gloria couldn't help falling in love with him, too.

In the photos they took of this son of the desert (who, in his boyhood, supposedly made a yearly journey across the Sahara to Timbuktu with his brothers, their camels, and their tents) his face shines in the sun, laughing, with brilliant white teeth. A free man! Whatever happened down there, George brought Gloria back safe and sound but then didn't stay long.

Gloria was filled with restlessness. Fear drove her forward. The semester break had barely begun when we were flying in the direction of the North Pole. Even as we took off, I could sense it was not going to be a long trip. We landed on Spitsbergen. But she couldn't stand the cold. Her teeth kept chattering and the hopeless, lost look returned to her face. By now, her beautiful features had grown completely stiff and immobile. After a few days, we flew back. When I told her we were returning early, she just shrugged her shoulders. Back in our apartment, Gloria summoned all her remaining strength.

"I know what you think, Christie. I know what you want to tell me. If not today, then tomorrow or the day after. But remember what you promised? Never again, never again!"

Then came the trip I had feared the most.

I was in a kind of trance, able to do only what she willed. I wasn't reacting in a normal way, I know. Even the pain had disappeared. The evening before we left, she said casually, "I'm going out for a little while. I just want to stop by my parents for a few minutes to say goodbye."

The next morning we flew to London and took the connecting flight to the Cayman Islands. Up in the clouds among the other, peacefully dozing passengers, she said, "I got stuck in the elevator. And the air is running out." Then she laughed, laid back her head, and fell asleep.

Albert stood up and started pacing restlessly back and forth.

"I knew next to nothing about all that. No one told me what was going on or how serious her condition was. When Gloria stopped by our house on the eve of her departure to say goodbye, I wasn't at home. I was at Erwin's house, celebrating his birthday. And Ann wasn't feeling well, as so often recently. When I got home later, she said, 'Gloria's going on a trip. To the Caymans again, to do some more diving, I guess. I've warned her ten times that these long trips in her condition are crazy.

She knows very well that the doctors have strictly forbidden them. She didn't even listen to me and left very soon after getting here.' She acted obstinate, Ann said, seemed like a different person. Ann thought you were behind it, Christie. You had gained our trust in your ingratiating way and now you were showing your true face. Finally she said you would surely both be back soon, like last time."

Albert spoke in a low, controlled voice.

His hands were shaking more again and he tilted his head to one side. Christie didn't dare look at him.

"I came back alone. It didn't take long."

"You called us in the middle of the night to say she had drowned. When you got back you came to see us very briefly. You brought us the death certificate. But you didn't want to talk about it."

"That's right. I couldn't talk about it."

"And I was furious. I fathered this child and loved her from the first day. And then—a death certificate! That was all! What had I done wrong? What was I to do with my love now? Why was I being punished so? That was my only thought. But no farewell, not even a little thought, no nothing. What could I ever do with my love for her now? A cheap piece of paper: death by drowning . . . her body somewhere in the sea. I was supposed to believe that, like I was supposed to believe in God. I had no other information. Your daughter is a good swimmer, but she drowned. None of it made any sense, but I had to believe it. And you, Christie, you said nothing."

Stillness filled the room. Lena, sitting off to one side, stretched in her chair.

"Do you have to be told everything? Can't you understand—just a bit?"

"Yes, it's true. There's so little I understand."

His head fell forward.

Lena got up, come over, and slowly stroked his hair. He sat slumped in his chair with tears running down his face.

"It's true, I said nothing!" Christie's voice sounded almost shrill. "But it's also true that every word would have stuck in my throat. I accompanied your daughter to her death . . . and you tell me I didn't say anything. What do you want from me?"

He lifted his head, then turned and looked Christie in the face.

"No, no. I didn't mean you. I'm getting everything confused. I meant . . . don't listen to me. . . ."

Lena went over to Christie. "Finish your story now, Christie. Then you can put it behind you. That's what you've come to us from so far away to do, isn't it?"

"Yes," Christie answered. She had calmed down again. "That's what I said. And you're right, Lena. The story's almost over. There are only a few more pages."

And she continued.

Stiff from the transatlantic flight, we transferred from the giant bird to a tiny, rickety plane. It was just a hop, skip, and jump and George was already standing there waiting for us with his Jeep by the wooden shack next to the grass landing strip. Today, in retrospect, I think he already guessed what would happen. We were back on our sleepy little island, remote from the rest of the world. We stayed in the same bungalow as before. The only difference was that George no longer came to us at night. Gloria lay beneath the glittering night sky and talked to herself while I tried to fall asleep inside.

Although Gloria hadn't spoken to either me or George, we knew. There was no need for superfluous talk. But I still hoped that it would all vanish into thin air—perhaps at the last moment. Maybe a miracle would happen!

And it seemed that way at first. A few days after our arrival, Gloria's face brightened up. She gave me an affectionate look. But then she had said to George and me, "Let's go diving tomorrow!" I suddenly realized I'd been waiting for this signal for weeks, days, hours, ever since the word "Caymans" had been uttered. "Caymans" and "diving." From her lips. That night, she lay down next to me, pressed her head against my shoulder, and took my hand as she always did.

"Why are you crying?"

"I don't know," I answered.

I was a coward. I couldn't get out anything else. I was helpless, paralyzed, despairing.

"All right, not tomorrow. We won't go diving tomorrow."

Again I thought, Now we're saved. I didn't ask why and for how long. I only knew: now we were saved, for the time being at least, and I fell asleep on the spot, exhausted.

We didn't go diving the next day. And we didn't go diving the day after that. We were only a few steps from the waves but we didn't touch the water. On the third day, I saw that George was packing up our diving gear and taking it to the boat, tight-lipped and impassive. As he passed me, he said offhandedly, "Are you coming too?"

I had no choice. Of course I was coming too! A few minutes later, I was sitting beside the two of them in George's boat. We puttered peacefully around the western tip of the island, looking down into the water that was calm and clear on this early morning. You could see a long way down. We went on and on and finally tied up to a remote buoy. No boat, no person in sight far and wide. Silently we got ready to jump into the water.

We put on the skintight wet suits, helped one another strap on the weights and shoulder the oxygen tanks. We put on our masks and put the mouthpiece into our mouths. The motor had stopped puttering quite a while ago. The silence was almost unbearable. The boat kept bumping restlessly against the buoy. We put on our flippers and jumped in feet first as we had been taught. George seemed nervous. He knew he was taking a big chance and possibly putting his beloved business at risk. I couldn't look at Gloria in the last minutes before we jumped, could hardly keep sitting upright I felt so miserable.

Gloria splashed in first and I landed right beside her. George followed. When we reached the bottom and the end of the mooring chain, fifty or sixty feet down, we leveled out horizontally and everything seemed as usual. But did any of us pay attention to the beauty all around us? I saw nothing—no fish, no rocks, no shells, no coral. The bottom we swam across fell away gently, almost imperceptibly. I didn't look at the little gauge that dangled from my chest. I didn't want to know how far we had come down. Nor did I pay any attention to the time or to my tank. Suddenly there it was: the wall. As if from a mountain ridge, we had a clear view down into the abyss. The blue changed to green, then farther down into a night blue that in another hundred meters merged into complete blackness. Schools of fish swam by. Proliferating coral and wild rock formations beckoned from the depths. I couldn't tear my eyes away. Here the wall dropped thousands of meters. We were swimming on the peak of a mountain of vast proportions.

With a few kicks I moved to the head of our group. My hands were clasped together, as we had been taught.

Everything seemed suddenly easy. The hopelessness and the terrible fear seemed to disappear. Like a bolt from the blue, I was overwhelmed with a feeling of happiness. I felt utter safety in the embrace of the sea. No one could see us, no one. We were all on our own and all was well.

All was well, no matter what happened. We were in the hands of eternity. What did our doubts, fears, and hardships count for? Thy will be done, I thought. Thy will. No—I didn't think it; the thought struck me. We kept swimming, now past gigantic circular rock formations that looked like they had been sculpted by human hands. Fantastic beings from a mysterious underworld. I reached out and touched their rounded, regular grooves. Large, sad-eyed fish emerged from the wall of coral and looked at me. Just beyond, a grotto opened up. Now George was in the lead, slightly above us with me behind him. With a few kicks of our flippers and our arms pressed against our sides we glided into a tunnel. The roof was so low that we had to pull in our heads. We left the sunlit water behind us. Just keep breathing calmly now! Why was George swimming so slowly? I couldn't get past him. The danger lying in wait for a diver is to get excited and lose control. I closed my eyes and tried to distract myself. I thought about my childhood, how I would kneel in the confession box with my hands folded in front of my face. Could God see me? Can he recognize me even here in the darkness of the sea? We emerged from the tunnel, farther down, more than a hundred feet already. My fear returned as quickly as it had left me.

Were we swimming deeper? We dropped down the wall, past stones, plants, and giant corals, past fantastic formations from Hieronymus Bosch. I saw Gloria below me. She was swimming calmly, seemed relaxed. How deep was she? A hundred feet was deep enough. A hundred twenty was the absolute limit, the borderline. We were getting too deep. Where was George?

Gloria looked up. Her eyes were enlarged by the glass of the mask, the pupils big, gigantic, penetrating. I dove a few strokes deeper, reached out toward her. Slowly, she lifted her right hand and made a circular gesture as if waving to me. I grabbed her hand and she swam close to me. We held each other tight for a few seconds, then she let go of my outstretched hand, dropped her head and her torso, and let herself sink deeper and deeper down the rock wall. The sunlight above her struck far into the sea. Beneath her was the twilight, farther down darkness, and finally blackness.

The depths drew me down too. I was filled with an irresistible desire to let myself sink along with her, farther and farther, deeper and deeper, not to leave her, to follow her down to where happiness resides. No longer to think, but to dream, to sleep, to forget. The feeling of happiness was boundless.

My body was shaken by a powerful jolt. A fist had grabbed me from behind and I was being pulled upward in strong strokes, violently, brutally. George didn't let go of me until we were hanging onto the mooring chain beneath our boat, waiting for our breathing to slow down before swimming the rest of the way to the surface. He shoved me once more, sending me upwards.

Afterwards, he didn't say a word. He left me to lift the heavy tank into the boat by myself and pull the weights off my waist with trembling hands. I clambered over the gunnel and crawled across the planks toward the bow like a dying animal. I couldn't lift my head. I rolled onto my back, stared straight into the blazing sun, and lost consciousness.

After we had landed, the silence brought me back to my senses. The bow had been pulled up on the sand and the boat still rocked slightly. George had disappeared and our equipment was gone too, even the tanks. I was alone. I was alone the rest of the day. After dark, George came into the bungalow and silently lay down next to me. That was all. In the middle of the night, I said, "Thank you." But he had already left again.

I had to stay on the island another three or four days. On the next day two police officers showed up in a boat from Cayman Brac and questioned us for hours. George explained how the accident had happened and I had only to nod in agreement. George was risking everything. His whole life was at stake. He repeatedly reconstructed the incident for them. Gloria, who was swimming behind the two of us, had gotten separated without us noticing. She'd probably lost her orientation. In distress George admitted that he hadn't reacted quickly enough. It was only a matter of seconds. Had anything like this happened to him before? Never! And he'd been doing this for a long time. Maybe her equipment had malfunctioned. Maybe the victim had reacted in some incorrect way. It was hard to reconstruct. Then they asked about her health. She was a sensitive person, delicate, but healthy. That was our testimony, and nothing else was known. She had probably run out of air and was too weak or too far away to signal for help.

It took them forever to write it all down. But a death is a death. Thank goodness such accidents almost never happened in the scuba divers' paradise, they said. Only once every dozen years or so, and they didn't like to make them public. After all, the good name of the islands was at stake. George cited his good—in fact, exemplary—reputation. He had lived here for years, was well known as a diving instructor, trusted as one of the very best. They interviewed a number of divers who had taken lessons from him and they all gave him the highest marks. Finally, we had to go to the police station on Cayman Brac to sign the transcript of our testimony, putting the seal on the tragedy with our signatures. We left the station with an official document that declared the death an accidental drowning. George and I couldn't look each other in the eye. And we never spoke again about the biggest lie of our lives.

Back home I plunged back into my medical studies, passed the state examination, and was officially a doctor. But I couldn't stand working in a hospital for long. I needed to get away.

And so I went to Africa where they greeted me with open arms. Since then, I've worked in medical centers and mostly in mobile clinics. I help wherever I can, treating infected eyes and ears, trying to ease pain, feed the starving, heal the sick, save lives. Too often, it's a hopeless undertaking.

George visited me there once. Because of his blond hair, all my colleagues and the nurses thought he was my brother. The color of our hair is in fact almost identical, and Gloria's was too. So he became my brother. He told me how he had left the Caymans very soon after the incident. He needed to get away. He tried working on the Maldive Islands but it was no better. Gloria and her death were always on his mind. He gave up being a diving instructor and started traveling. He crossed India from the far north down to the southern tip, visiting its beaches and bays and the Kerala backwaters.

For a few weeks he lent a hand at our medical station, changing bandages, dispensing medications, and working in the kitchen.

One day he asked me, "Would you like to live together?"

"How could we do that, George?" I answered. "I can't replace anyone for you."

"Not like that, Christie. I meant as brother and sister."

"Okay," I said, "if you want to."

Weeks went by. The night before he left, we made love. Neither of us had planned it, it just happened. Our bodies found each other, had come to some arrangement without asking our permission. It was a wonderful night, half dream and half reality. As he entered me, the tears streamed down my cheeks. We were lying in a big tent under mosquito netting. Strange birds were cawing nearby. Our shared grief had brought us together. Then calls in the distance and the snorting of animals. What difference did it make to us? We didn't let go of each other for a single second. My body was glowing. It was already getting light when we finally fell asleep, totally exhausted as after a long, victorious struggle. Was Gloria with us even though not a thought of her had crossed my mind? I think she was.

She was always with us when we were together.

Then I dreamed of her. At the edge of the desert I dreamed of the depths of the sea. But it was a beautiful dream. Everything was peaceful: the fish, the coral, the undulating green plants, shiny and slippery, on the crumbling stone. When I woke up, he kissed me once more, then he was gone.

Later, his father died and George took over the family farm in Australia, not far from the coast. He called me from down there and said excitedly, "Perhaps you'll come for a visit. It's beautiful here. You'd like it."

"We'll see," I answered. "Maybe for a visit. . . ."

"Maybe for even longer. Come to the new world!"

"What's your idea? What would I do there?"

"I mean later, maybe. There's a need for doctors here, too. And then perhaps we could . . ."

"What?"

"Well, we could have children."

"Children?" I laughed out loud. "That's the last thing on my mind."

And that's all I said.

Then came the day of departure. Christie's flight to Africa was scheduled to leave. They had only a few more hours.

At breakfast she said, "Albert, you asked yesterday what you could do with your love for her. Why don't you to go the sea? It's not that far away."

"To the sea? Why there?"

"That's where your daughter is buried. Other people go to the cemetery and put flowers on a grave. Why not throw a bouquet onto the water? The waves will carry it away."

"Should I?"

"The sea is the greatest cemetery on earth. Go to the coast, throw the flowers onto the water and you'll be laying them on Gloria's grave."

They kissed each other goodbye. Albert kissed her on the mouth as he had always kissed his daughter and stammered, "Thank you."

He and Lena waved goodbye as Christie drove up the narrow unpaved drive toward the edge of the woods where they had walked so often in the past days. They watched until the car turned onto the road in a cloud of dust and slowly was lost to view.

Albert stood beside Lena. Christie was gone, Christie who had been around him since she was a girl, Gloria's sister.

She was almost a part of him. He was so grateful for these days with her, grateful she had finally told him the truth about his daughter's death. But what about Lena, her mother? Now that her daughter was gone, Lena seemed like a stranger to him. He didn't know what to do now, what to say. Wasn't it time for him to leave as well? Why hadn't he left with Christie? Irresolutely he followed Lena as she walked slowly, pensively toward the edge of the woods. When they reached the trees, he was beside her. He saw the clouds part and the sun appear. Its warmth did him good.

"A beautiful day," he heard himself say.

"All days are beautiful here. I don't grade them. It's good to be out in nature. No, I don't miss the city and its noise, all those people. I'm a lot better since I've been living here."

Albert thought about what she had said. He was silent as they entered the twilight of the woods. They stopped and listened like children to a cuckoo's call. That pleased him. But what he liked most of all was the anthill, "his" anthill as he called it. Lena didn't contradict him. She smiled. They both looked down at the ant colony and watched the insects swarming out of their huge, delicately structured hill, making their way through the underbrush that surrounded it, marching in columns, one behind the other. And in other columns came other ants returning home. Some carried heavy loads larger than their tiny bodies, fir sprigs that would be piled onto the hill. All the identical little creatures with the same mission: to work, to labor, to be part of a great, inextricable whole. But who assigned them their tasks? Who sent them on their way? Who was in charge of this unending bustle, this assiduous labor for some invisible reward? And why? What about mankind, he asked himself. What about me? Who gave me my assignment? Am I a part of an inextricable whole?

They sat down on a nearby wooden bench, leaned back comfortably, and breathed in the smell of the forest.

"We've had some long days. Now I don't have to ask any more questions," said Albert.

Lena sat close beside him. "Now you can sleep peacefully, as much as you like."

They both smiled while she stroked the back of his hand with hers.

three

Fragmentary images flew past. For the last leg of the return trip, Ann had taken the high-speed train. She was feeling no discomfort, no, and of course it wasn't anxiety. Once the initial prickly feeling in her legs subsided, she was suffused by an unexpected sense of well-being. She was floating, distanced from her surroundings. It's better than flying, she thought.

She was glad the seat across from her was empty. The passengers facing her looked weary, drowsy, one or two looked worried. No one smiled. Do I like my fellow man? Do I still like them, she asked herself. It seems I've become alienated. Her sister's message was crystal clear: Live in the present! Seek happiness before it's too late! No, in the days that had brought them back together Mary hadn't said it in so many words, but it was the message she radiated. A happy time, she thought. My Mary! She was far away for so long, but now? She had been so near, so empathetic, so loving. A sister! My only sister! Yes, they had finally found each other again, with Mary on her deathbed! Yes, I understood what she was trying to tell me. How strange to feel such deep sorrow and yet such happiness with her. It's not death that's terrible, it's life. So banish darkness and don't die before your time!

The train rolled slowly across the bridge. The river greeted her like an old friend. The cathedral appeared, office buildings. Then with a little jolt the train came to a stop. Ann had already stood up and started to collect her bags. She stepped out onto the platform and felt suddenly exhausted from the long trip. Was she home at last? Why was the station so deserted? She looked around. No one had come to pick her up. Anton had sent his regrets; he was on a business trip. But what about Albert? Shouldn't he be here, after all she'd been through? Where was he? Oh yes, that's right, he couldn't have known. . . . But if he had the strength to disappear into the country for days, then he could have been here now! The shock of the last few days was still in her bones.

Ann walked quickly through the station concourse, pulling her suitcase behind her. She had to think about what she'd expected. What did she want? Yes, that was it: expectations! Did she really have some claim on him, the right to have him here to meet her? She didn't know. She knew she should have asked herself this question sooner and not waited until now. Her daily concerns: caring for him, so many things that constitute her daily life and obscure what's important. One is quick to think one knows everything, has everything under control, including one's spouse. But in reality? Death raises so many questions. Her image of her sister was fixed in place for so many years, decades, already determined when they were young. And now: was she the same person? Did she resemble the image Ann had set in place so long, long ago? No! She certainly did not.

The air in the house seemed stale. There was no one here to welcome her either. Irma had already gone home, leaving a brief, businesslike message lying indifferently on the kitchen table. She unpacked, straightened a few pieces of furniture, went out to the garden for a moment. The day was sunny and the evening promised to be fair.

Later she sat at the little desk in her bedroom. Surprisingly, she felt rested and with no time to lose. Above all, her head was clear. She wanted to get it down, capture the fleeing thought. And sitting with her back straight and her head slightly inclined, she began to write:

Father taught me that when things get tough and you don't know how to go on—when a stranger looks back at you from the mirror—then you have to face up to it, not try to avoid it. If you do, he said, you'll go astray. God is always there, whether you want him or not. He's asking the questions and giving the assignments like a schoolteacher. He puts stumbling blocks in your way and sends the fallen angel Lucifer to mislead you. It's up to you not to lose sight of the way, up to you not to shirk your duty when you're asked something, when you have to take responsibility for something and there's a truth to be learned. Then take a pen and a sheet of good paper and write down your confession. Find yourself in the written word. But don't be smug! Put aside your self-love! Forget about yourself and examine the things that matter to you. Examine them from all sides, do you hear! Be your own judge! It can be painful—very painful, in fact. The house of cards you've constructed may well collapse. When you feel most despondent, you're closest to the truth. The truth is not free of charge, but you have to give it a chance. Write your fingers to the bone until you've reached the kernel of self-knowledge, even if it takes days, weeks, months.

Even if you grow old in the search. Why didn't Father say: Break free! It was my sister Mary who said it: Break free!

My father was a strong man, a guide both loved and feared. No one in my entire life was his equal. Truthfulness was his lodestar, nothing was more important; not truthfulness to men so much as truthfulness to God, though he was not a church-goer. Nevertheless, a Bible lay on his bedside table. The duty Father instilled in me didn't make my life easy. I was often sub-jected to the scorn, antipathy, and ridicule of schoolmates, of my sister when she rebelled against him, and of men I met as a young woman. Only Albert was different. I had to learn that everything has its price, that you have to pay for your convic-tions and your faith. Some lose heart and betray themselves. I hold such people in contempt. I can't help it and it's hard not to let it show. But I began to have doubts. Lying in bed at night, alone, my body on fire, I would secretly curse my father, curse him and then despise myself for it.

Mary is dead. I held her hand until the very end, the hand of my little sister, the woman who loved life. Now she's gone, tak-ing my childhood and my youth along with her. We had so much in common! The first Christmas I can remember, she lay in the cradle and Mother said, "She's our Christ child." Was I jealous of her? Or later, during the cherry harvest, we'd sit to-gether in the tree and stuff ourselves with fruit. The birthday parties with our little girlfriends from the neighborhood, or when we crawled into each other's bed at night to cuddle and tell each other stories under the blanket, quietly, so our parents wouldn't find out. We shared all our secrets and important news—things long since forgotten! Later, we parted ways and what we had in common was displaced by what separated us. We started criticizing each other, something that would have been unthinkable before. Then finally, at the end of our long journey, our paths met again and I was allowed to be there during her final days, she looked at me in the old familiar way and all barriers vanished. I saw my little sister again, found my way back to her. Her death returned a fragment of understanding to me: sympathy, above all, and the cruel realization that I had become arrogant, hardened, and misanthropic. I fear the time has come to indict myself.

As Mary lay dying and I had to go and be with her, Christie appeared unexpectedly on our doorstep and took Albert away to her mother's in the country. At first I thought it was just a day's excursion, but then his absence was extended and I began to have my doubts. Would they take proper care of the sick man, look after him as he was used to from me? On the telephone I begged him to return home, but he wanted to stay. Why, I wonder? That's not my Albert. What made him take such a step? But be honest, do you have an exclusive right to care for him? Is he my property? Isn't anyone else allowed to get close to him? Or have I been seized by jealousy?

Mary is gone and I've come back today. I'm sitting alone in an empty house waiting for him. I hear the kitchen clock strike, but he doesn't come. Albert's been gone for over a week now. Yes, I was gone myself, but for a sad and urgent reason. What about him? And now I'm back and he knows I am, but he's still not here. Does he think I don't need him at my side after the difficult days I've been through? Doesn't he know he should be supporting me now, sharing my grief? Obviously, my pain doesn't bother him.

I'm afraid to spend the night all alone in this house. It's so quiet! I'll wander from room to room, complaining and angry, and won't be able to sleep until the early morning hours.

Tomorrow I'll ask Irma about Albert and how he was feeling in the days before he left. Supposedly he was in good spirits,
expansive, went out shopping! And there was a certain triumph
in Irma's voice when she told me that on the telephone. It's obvious she's on his side.

I think of my father. I think of him often though he's been
dead so long. Never forget, he told me, no one is your property,
not your father or your mother or your sister. Not even your
children, to say nothing of your husband. If anything belongs
to you, it's your own self, and even that you must share with
God. And in the end, He's the one who makes the decisions,
the boss!

So, does Albert belong to me? I've waited on him and cared for
him when he got sick. I think I gave him priority over my own
interests and wishes. Travel was postponed, our usual trips to
the festivals in Salzburg and Bayreuth were gradually dropped.
How I loved our days there: the music, the glamour of those
places. I couldn't bring it up with Albert anymore and I told myself he was sick and I'd have to sacrifice my wishes. Maybe I
even said that out loud sometimes, which I now regret.

I ask myself now if my constant devotion to duty made me
hard. With my duty to take care of him, did I also begin making Albert into a possession without consciously meaning to,
little by little?

What does Christie want with Albert? It's true, we used to feel
close to her. But later, we grew distant. But she always stood by

Albert. She stayed true to him, if not to me, right up to Gloria's death. I came more and more to suspect that she, Christie, wanted to take our daughter from us. She was positively obsessed with the notion of becoming one with Gloria, of having her completely to herself. Gloria's parents were the losers in that game, although Albert was blind to it.

And now? Is she playing the same game? Except now it's Albert she wants to turn against me? He was never like this before. And what about Lena? What role is the mysterious, inscrutable Lena playing? She's been living out there by herself for a long time. And she likes Albert, that's for sure. Am I mistaken? Am I seeing things—dark, threatening clouds—before they even appear? Has my brain been addled by my sister's death? Still, what does Lena want?

No, no. The whole thing has made me hard. They took my daughter from me, my only daughter. It was just little things at first, hardly noticeable. I was too good-natured and fell into the trap. Albert and Christie were soon at work, in league with each other, step by step until Gloria wouldn't even look at me, her own mother. Her ears were closed to my words of love and concern, words born in the nights I spent weeping about her. The trap had closed. She was available to everyone—Albert, Christie, her friends. And then the lovers who came and went, took possession of her and stole her away, the hordes of doctors, each one a know-it-all without a soul and without pity. Gloria's long trips to every corner of the world. They all pushed her, gave her challenges, regarded her as a plaything or a trophy. They were so thoughtless, so unreasonable. And who had to pay the price? Not Albert, not Christie or any of the others. No, Ann did. I did! With my flesh and blood, with the life of my daughter, that wonderful creature, so beautiful and precious. Even Father was overcome by the sweet little being for the few years he knew her.

I have to think, to keep thinking! Is it really the way my emotions tell me? Can it be so? Is it really true that life takes from you and you have no say in it? Is there ever a victim who wasn't secretly in league with the perpetrator? Perhaps without realizing it, but with the yearning of his soul. Don't hurt me, don't touch me, but take me!

Haven't I learned, just now at Mary's deathbed, that everything is different at the end? You realize with a shudder that your one-sided accounts and ill-starred expectations never work out. The calculations you've been working on for half your life refuse to come out even. Your hopes were pinned on a worthless scrap of paper, trash. Trash, like so many other things!

There are no accounts without offsets. Life is one great accounting of the exchange of goods. But who closes the deal in the end?

On the telephone Albert told me that he was spending time with Christie to learn the details of Gloria's death. Our repeated, painful fumbling in the dark was bad enough and now it would finally end. The truth would be sad, very sad, but at last it would bring us some light. And he would tell me about it. Is that what Christie planned? She could have waited until after Mary's death. Did it just happen to coincide? Hard to imagine. On the other hand, I had turned away from Christie and thought she had betrayed me. I was filled with reproach toward her. Is it possible I did her an injustice?

Of course, I have to face the possibility that Albert doesn't love me anymore. I always thought he would be grateful for everything I've done for him. But does the expectation of gratitude have anything to do with love? It's just another deal! Shouldn't we do good from selfless impulse? If you put conditions on doing good, it's just a business deal. But a business deal in a marriage? Again, an account with an offset! A terribly wrong path! No, that's not how I want to be. And yet I let myself be tempted down that path, step by step. For God's sake! If that's how it is, then I'm ashamed of myself. My long-dead father would have given me the dressing-down I deserve, or Albert will do it now!

We loved each other. I loved Albert with all my heart when we got married. He was a gorgeous man with bright blue eyes, blond hair—a wild mane of it back then—a confident step, and an open, reassuring smile without a hint of caution. A man who believed in goodness despite all of life's setbacks. A man who made me feel safe, whom I could depend on. He was Father's closest colleague, loyal, circumspect, hardworking. He began as his assistant, then became his agent, and finally his successor. But what became of our love? I don't know. It was like a dress made of feathers that disintegrates, the feathers gently floating to the floor one by one, unnoticed at first, silently, until they cover the floor beneath you and you trample them underfoot and suddenly stand there naked and complaining at the top of your lungs. But why? Whose fault was it?

I think I was prepared for everything, for sickness, failure, forgetfulness, but not for the passing of time. Time defeated us without ever identifying itself as our opponent. It stole in at night on silent feet and made itself at home. Can you catch hold of time, shake it, wrestle with it, beat it back, or even overcome

it? I don't know. And even if you could, would I have the strength
to do it? Wouldn't it take two of us, two who wanted to defeat
time together? But how? With what weapons? It's not so simple
after all. Quite the opposite.

You'd need a shared determination and then something
else, something I hardly dare to mention or write down. For
what seems to come naturally when you are young looks like
a miracle to me today: affection, trust, tenderness—love. In
freedom! You didn't think about it back then. You never did.
You never clearly understood what life's greatest mystery is.
You took everything for granted. How frivolous you were, how
ungrateful! My God, what must I do to get back to the source,
back to my true self? Where am I, how did I lose my way? Did I
forfeit the miracle through my thoughtlessness, my indifference, forfeit it forever?

My God, I was young once, wasn't I? With all the yearn-
ings and passions that overwhelmed me like a hot desert wind.
My father tried to counteract all that. Control yourself! Don't
throw yourself away. Stay cool. Don't take risks you may regret
later. But the more I obeyed Father, the more I burned with
desire. Later, when I married Albert, I stumbled blindly into
married life. Was I always honest with him? Did I always let
him know what I was really like? No, I showed him only the
side of me that Father said I should. Wasn't that too little? From
the very beginning, wasn't I cheating him and myself of the
very heart of love, which is trust?

Anton, our devoted Anton, has offered to drive out to Lena's
and have a heart-to-heart talk with his father—straighten the
old man out, as he put it. That would only make things worse,
for heaven's sake, break even more china! I asked him to drop

the idea and pay more attention to Lori instead. That would please his father the most. He should leave Albert to me.

Days have passed and Albert still isn't back. He's been at Lena's for what seems an eternity and I hear that Christie has already left. She stopped to see Lori before catching the plane to Africa. Anton got to see her before her departure. He told me enthusiastically that Christie looked gorgeous and said how warmly she spoke of her time with Albert. I hope Anton hasn't fallen in love with her again!

But why is Albert still out in the country? What business does he have to be there? I haven't heard a peep out of him.

But I want him back now, now that Christie has left! And then there's Lena—Lena the mild, the modest, the friendly. She's obviously good for him. I only met her a few times, but her image is engraved in my memory—patient, understanding, and apparently undemanding. A good listener. Unlike me? What can I counter with? My taking care of him, certainly. But is it enough just to look after him physically? The soul withers, loneliness grows from day to day. What did I give him? Was it enough? He came to depend more and more on my help. I made it clear to him that he couldn't survive without me. But I'm not his only support anymore. And he won't come back to me un-less I show him I love him. In all these years the marriage bond has hardened into habit and duty. Get rid of all that! Break the bonds! Now with my sister in the grave, the scales are falling from my eyes.

· · ·

It's clear now that Lena is my rival, not Christie. As much as it hurts to say so, I have to face the truth. Lena seems to be a fairly simple soul, but is she also calculating? I must measure myself against her. If I just ignore her or even hate her, I've lost. I have to get hold of her, ask to meet with her. Just the two of us. I hope she will agree to see me.

four

They're listening to music her daughter brought back from one of her trips, and it's impossible to stay in their seats. Albert jumps up and Lena is right beside him like a girl who can guess exactly what he wants. The woman's singing—full of longing and desire—has them in its spell. With his left hand, the old man takes hold of her right hand and puts his other arm around her waist. He lifts his foot to take the first step. His back is straight and his face tilted upwards. He has a boyish smile that radiates great peacefulness and concentration. His hands have stopped shaking. She's a head shorter than he. When he looks down, he can see the straight part that seems to divide her into two halves from above. Although she often moves a bit ponderously, as she takes the first steps with him now she seems light and agile. It's marvelously easy to lead her. They are perfect partners right from the start. He thinks it and feels it too, without a doubt. He pulls her closer to him and feels the warmth of her body through her thin, long dress—as if she were wearing nothing underneath.

Albert raises his left arm up as far as her right arm can extend. She moves closer to him and they glide, turn, and twirl across the room, floating in each other's arms, while the voice repeats, "*Que mos travers, caminos es camino pasando me. Sodar, sodar, sodar.*"

It seems to go on forever. Finally, Lena drops her arms and

pushes the exhausted but still dancing Albert into an armchair. The forward momentum makes her lose her balance and with a squeal of delight, she falls onto his lap. Flushed and happy, the two of them can't hold in their liberating laughter. Gasping for breath, Lena lays her head on Albert's shoulder and he pants, "It's a secret language: longing . . . longing . . . longing for my São Nicolau . . . longing for São Nicolau."

"And how does it go on from there?"

"If you write me, I'll write you. If you forget me, I'll forget you until the day you come back. Longing . . . longing . . . longing for my São Nicolau."

"And it's a secret language?"

"At least, it's not all Portuguese. As Christie told it, a heavy-set woman stood immobile onstage and sang it. She was longing for . . ."

"For what?"

"For an island in Cape Verde, a place strangers hardly ever set foot on."

They listen happily to the music. Albert gently pushes her off his lap and stands up, then they fall into each other's arms again and their legs move to the rhythm of the song. Lena looks up at him with a radiant smile. "You're a marvelous dancer! Who would have guessed?"

"This reminds me of the time I danced down the entire Copacabana from one end to the other. The whole Copacabana!"

"You danced down the entire Copacabana?"

"Of course I did, many times . . . many . . ."

Lena looks up skeptically. "Many times?"

Albert falls silent, then finally says, "Of course I did. Don't you believe me? You women are all doubting Thomases."

"I believe whatever you say, Albert."

He's thinking again. They come to a standstill. "Let me think for a minute. . . . Now I know how it was. Of course, as I said . . . but it's not just reality that exists, the imagination does too! I dreamed it a hundred times. Those were the years when my dreams were what was real to me."

"And now?"

"Now you're what's real. But I don't know if you're a dream or reality. Do you, Lena? Maybe you can help an old man."

"No, dear Albert, I can't. How should I know if I'm a dream or reality for you? But whichever it is, you can touch me."

"I'll touch you, I'll hug you, I'll hold you tight, Lena. But there's no one to tell me if I'm dreaming or not. I think you're a dream, Lena."

She pulls her head back and looks him in the eye.

"I'm reality. But I don't mind if you think I'm a dream. I don't mind at all. And it doesn't bother me to give you a kiss I dreamed about a hundred years ago."

They stand in a long embrace. She's made herself light as a feather for him. Her mouth is on his mouth, and finally his legs give way and they slide to the floor.

Perspiring and wearing nothing but his pajama pants, his arms and legs trembling, he stands in front of a mirror and sees a man he doesn't know, a stranger looking back at him. But the stranger looking at him with such surprise doesn't make him uneasy. In fact, he thinks he could get to like him. Lena untied his shoes for him in the living room, unbuttoned his shirt and pants. How he loves it when she pampers him like a child.

Albert shuffles the short distance to his little bedroom. From the darkened room, he peers through the window into the moonlit garden. The little firs and the bushes cast sharply outlined shadows onto the lawn. In the shadows, a ghostly figure is moving back and forth. She lifts her arms like an ancient priestess, dances a few steps in a circle in animated imitation of what she just danced with him. He holds his breath and stares openmouthed at this apparition, separated from him only by the thin windowpane. Before his astonished eyes she sheds her clothing, one garment at a time. The image flutters like an old silent film that threatens at any moment to tear or burn through. He sees the outline of her body through her blouse, then she reveals her naked body to his yearning gaze. O kindly moonlight, pale and bright, when at last the dark clouds drift away! Her silhouette, her bare feet, her legs, hips, torso, shoulders, breasts and neck! Near enough to touch! How slim and girlish she is! As he stretches out his arms to her, the figure is gone as quickly as it appeared. He leans his forehead on the glass and searches the moonlit, nocturnal garden in vain. Dark shadows lie on the grass. The queen of the night has been eclipsed. He moves the short distance to his bed, stretches out weary limbs that won't settle down. Because I'm happy, he thinks. After a few minutes, he's enfolded in a deep sleep that won't release him for a good long while.

In the night, he thinks he feels a warm body pressing softly, gently against his. A breath falls on his face. A small hand—a woman's hand, a mother's hand—covers his mouth, brushes over his closed eyes and pauses on his forehead, glides over his ear and across his neck to his bare chest, becomes entangled in its hair, strokes his rib cage, and comes to rest on his rounded belly that has stopped moving up and down with his breath.

For a long time, they lay like that without a word, side by side, body by body, skin next to skin, hardly daring to breathe, motionless except for her hand that fondles him again and again. Finally he turns to her, pulls her close, and pauses a moment before they become indissolubly one.

Albert woke up late the following day. She was gone. A note on the breakfast table said she had driven to the nearby town. He shouldn't worry, she'd be back before noon. And there it was in black and white, in her clear schoolgirl's hand, "Kisses, Lena." Although he was surprised that she had left, the last two words of her note were so reassuring he began to sing and dance around the house. But how clumsy his steps were! Without her he felt hobbled, crippled. The images of yesterday evening and last night became sharper minute by minute, until he couldn't hold it in any longer: "I'm alive, alive, alive!"

While Albert was shouting out his joy, Lena has reached town in the rattling old Ford she steers with the intense concentration of someone who doesn't drive often. The twelve-mile drive had taken her a good half hour, annoying several more impatient drivers along the way. Lena was relieved to find a free parking spot next to a shiny Mercedes, across the street from the Hotel zur Post. Still sitting behind the wheel, she combed her windblown hair, reapplied her lipstick, and checked the placement of the brooch that pinned her silk blouse together at the breast. Then she inspected the results of her work in the mirror on the back of her visor. She took her time. She was not in a hurry. She had nothing to lose. Last night seemed to her the high point of recent years, perhaps of her entire life! No one could take last night from her, not even Ann—who was probably already in the hotel, waiting impatiently. Last night belonged to her, irrevocably and forever. She could just sit here, then turn around, drive back home, and embrace Albert. Secure in the knowledge of her good fortune, however, of the great gift she had received, she was so brimful of happiness that she had no fear of compromising it. A last look at her reflection in the little mirror, then she opened the door, got out, and locked the car. She'd had it for years and it had served her well and never let her down. Soon after Jakob's death, she had signed up for driving lessons and had grown old with this car she'd become so fond of. She used it to move out here from town. Such were her thoughts as she looked right and left and then crossed the street, entered the hotel, and asked for Ann. When she finds her, she will look her in the eye and extend her hand. She was ten minutes late for their appointment. Perfect! There was only one thing she had to watch out for. She absolutely must not betray how happy she is. She had to banish any trace of joy from her face: not the slightest smile, not the smallest twinkle is permitted. As long as the meeting with Ann lasted, no matter what they talked about, she'd be forced to play the Lena she'd always played, ever since she was a girl. She must extinguish last night from her memory, at least for the next hour. On the drive back, she can rekindle it all the brighter.

The woman standing so straight and tall in the little foyer of the provincial hotel was Ann, no doubt about it. Albert's wife and Gloria's mother looked the way she remembered her from their few, brief encounters years ago. Ann has aged, she thinks.

The expression on her face, however, was not what she expected. It was less hard, more friendly, unpretentious, and sadder than she'd thought. Where's the unbending dictator she was anticipating. Doesn't she look younger? She looks younger than me, but is she happy? Of course, she did lose her sister just a few days ago. That's why she's wearing black, and she looks great in it. And then, she has a tough row to hoe. She's lost her husband Albert! And Albert was back at her house, Lena's house. And she spent the night with him, side by side in bed, lying in his arms with his pajama pants balled up between his legs.

They greeted each other formally, almost ceremoniously. Both had dressed up for the occasion, as if by agreement. No, this was no everyday appointment. It was an encounter that will demand negotiation. Both of them were all too aware of that. After all, it was about a man, "their" man, who at this moment was sitting in Lena's kitchen without a care in the world, putting a piece of bread and jam into his mouth. No slipups now! Don't show your cards too soon! That's what both of them were thinking, the tall, slim, straight-backed Ann and the smaller, plumper Lena.

They sat down at a small table on one side of the foyer and ordered tea from a waitress. Ann opened the conversation, "First, I'd like to thank you for agreeing to come when I phoned. May I call you Lena?"

"Please do," Lena answered quickly. "We've known each other a long time and there's so much we have in common from those years."

"You're right. It's been decades, but we've never . . ."

"Gotten to know each other well. On the contrary, I think we only met two or three times, if I recall, and that was long ago."

Ann folded her hands.

"My God, we were so preoccupied with our own affairs, at least Albert and I were. All our concerns about Gloria—they never let up. And your daughter Christie was such a big, big help to us. She took over looking after Gloria completely. I'm afraid we didn't think enough about the effects on you, Lena. We weren't paying enough attention. I regret that very much. But it's a little late for regrets, I admit."

"We move in different circles."

Ann looked intently at the woman sitting across from her. Could this be a trap? She must be cautious.

"We shared our daughters. I'd like to thank you again for that. It meant more than I can express in words. It's too bad that later our paths diverged. It was very painful for us, for Albert and me."

Lena didn't respond. She looked past Ann and sipped her tea slowly—provocatively slowly, as if giving Ann time to make a mistake. And indeed: Ann's barely maintained façade slipped visibly.

"For us, everything was much more painful than any on-looker can imagine. Gloria's condition was getting worse every day. Her stays in the clinic were hell for us, absolute hell! It's impossible for an outsider to fully understand."

"I wasn't an outsider."

"No, of course not! And then those trips the two of them went on! They were so unreasonable, so irresponsible! Against the doctors' advice! I sometimes think we could have saved Gloria if the two of them—she and Christie—hadn't withdrawn from us."

Ann began to cry, fumbled in her purse for a tissue to wipe her eyes.

Lena got up, calm and collected as always, walked around the table to Ann, and laid her hand on her shoulder. "Don't be sad. It was God's will. And—I didn't feel I should say this first thing—my condolences on your sister's death. That must have grieved you very deeply."

Ann stood up as if called to attention. How can this woman have such a strong effect on her? How does Lena manage to stir her up so much with just a few words? She allowed Lena to give her a brief hug of sympathy before sitting back down.

Lena also sat down and straightened out her skirt. "I wasn't an onlooker."

"No one said you were. I never meant to say so, never!" I'm so emotional, Ann thinks to herself. I helplessly snap up every scrap she throws me. Why didn't I remain silent?

Lena had ordered a glass of fruit juice after the tea and now drank it with obvious pleasure. She seemed to be feeling fine.

"Please forgive me for not coming to see you in town, Ann. I would have liked to see what you've done with the house. Christie has told me so much about how beautiful it is. But the public transportation is so inadequate out here in the country that I'm dependent on my car. And to be honest, I'm a pretty hopeless driver. My husband absolutely forbade me to get a driver's license. He didn't trust me to do anything. I didn't learn to drive until after his death and I'm thankful if I can make it around the next corner with my old car."

Lena was surprised to hear a melody coming from Ann's purse. It proved to be her cell phone. Ann pressed a key. "Hello? Hello, Anton! I thought it might be you. . . . Yes, I'm fine. Why shouldn't I be? . . . It's nice out here in the country. . . . I already told you I'm fine. . . . Problems? Please! . . . Yes, don't

worry about me. . . . Maybe I'll see you this evening. . . . Until
then! . . . Yes, Anton. . . . Bye!"

The short conversation seemed to have restored Ann's equi-
librium.

"Does Albert know about our meeting?"

Now Lena was picking through her own large purse.

"Where did I put that? . . . No, Albert doesn't know anything. Should he? He's fine. . . . But I have something for you,
one of Gloria's notes. She had the peculiar habit of writing
down her thoughts on little slips of paper—peculiar because she
would then drop them on the floor and pay no more attention
to them, as if they'd ceased to exist. Christie saved a whole box
of them and she asked me to give you this one."

Quick as lightning, Ann took the piece of paper from Lena's
outstretched hand. It took her only a moment to read the short
text:

> *I don't want to die alone. I'm afraid to live and afraid to die. I live in*
> *a no-man's-land between life and death, in an elevator stuck be-*
> *tween floors and running out of air.*

Without another word, she put the slip into her purse, then
looked firmly at Lena.

"I have something for you, too, a letter to Albert. Would
you please . . ."

"You could give it to him yourself. Why not? It's not far
from here."

Lena saw her catch her breath. How sure of herself is Ann?
Is she as certain of Albert as she acts? Is she really a rival?

"Absolutely not!" Ann interrupted Lena's thoughts. "Please
take him the letter. I'd only frighten him if I showed up sud-

denly and unexpectedly. What do you think, Lena? When will
he come back to town? Has he said anything about his plans?
He was pretty monosyllabic on the telephone. Talking on the
phone was never his strong suit. What do you think?"

Ann flashed her a smile.

Lena leaned back in her chair and waved at a couple crossing the foyer.

"Please, Ann, what do you want me to do? I would never
presume . . . Albert is your husband! I've never in my life gotten mixed up in other people's affairs, to say nothing of their
marriages. It's not my way. That's a question between you and
Albert, don't you think?"

"Of course, of course. You're right. I just thought perhaps
you—"

Ann stopped. She looked at Lena, whose face seemed to her
to have assumed a sly expression. Again she waved to someone
crossing the little hotel foyer. Is that really necessary? Is she trying to be provocative, lure me out into the open?

"Are you listening to me, my dear?"

I shouldn't have said that, flashed through her mind. It
sounds too much like a rebuke. And then to add "my dear"! No,
this obviously wasn't her day! It sounded grotesque or worse,
with a sneering undertone. That was precisely how she didn't
intend to sound, quite the opposite! Obviously she was spoiling
her chances. But how could it be her day? First the pain of her
only sister's death, then the sudden, unexpected affront of her
husband leaving home the one time she really needed him.

As if from far away, she heard Lena's voice, "I think it's you
who aren't listening, Ann! Well, our thoughts . . ."

"Yes, you're right, Lena! Our thoughts . . . and . . . and how
is Albert, anyway? I forgot to ask . . ."

"The country air! I think the country air . . ."

"Ah, yes! Of course, the country air will do him good."

*A few minutes later, the two women were standing on the side-*walk between the shiny Mercedes and the old Ford. They didn't embrace again, just smiled briefly and pressed each other's hands for a long moment. What would Lena tell Albert about their meeting, Ann wondered. And Lena? He'll go back to her, flashed through her head. And: he's a decent man. That's why I love him. But must he be? I could forgive him for not being quite so decent.

When Lena pulled in the driveway, she had long since decided not to give him the letter right away—not today. Whatever may be in it, she was certainly not going to let Ann steal the rest of this valuable day from her. On the way back, she had bought a bottle of champagne. Where is Albert? She started looking around for him. The front door was wide open. He couldn't be far away. But she couldn't find him anywhere in the house or the garden. He hadn't left a note, nothing. Did he suddenly decide to hold her absence against her? To disappear so unexpectedly, so unannounced, after a night like theirs! Maybe he was evening the score by taking a taxi or the bus back to town. His clothes were still hanging in the wardrobe, but that didn't prove any-thing. It's hard to know what a man is thinking.

She called his name in a loud voice, again and again. Finally she dropped despondently onto the bench in front of the house and started to cry. She raised her solitary voice, complained, felt sorry for herself, and lamented until the tears began to fall. Has she lost him? While she cut a bold figure in her meeting with Ann and seemed to have won their duel, she now saw her hopes dashed. A trap . . . she indulged herself in mourning her beloved. Then suddenly she heard him, nearby, familiar, friendly, even loving, "How lovely to hear you! I think someone loves me and misses me."

Dumbfounded, she looked right and left, saw nothing, and finally looked up. He was sitting quite close in the big old apple tree, the eminence of her garden, with a straw hat on his head. The old man was perched where the trunk forked and shaking with laughter.

"I just wanted to see if I could still climb a damned apple tree in my old age without breaking my neck. And I also wanted to surprise you like you surprised me. It obviously succeeded perfectly."

She jumped to her feet.

"Oh, Lord, you old fool! You just go off and climb a tree! But don't move, please, it's okay with me if you stay right there."

"Thanks for your understanding! There's nothing better than to have a loving woman grant you your freedom. Things are looking up!"

"Yes, yes. I'll toss you a blanket later, when it gets cooler. You've got enough to eat up there. Enjoy the pleasant breezes. Meanwhile, I'm going to fry myself some eggs and potatoes."

"All right . . . your kindness is unparalleled! . . . I couldn't ask for more."

He kept stopping to laugh out loud.

"A night spent under the stars is a marvelous adventure! I envy you, little boy. How old are you? Twelve or thirteen?"

"Let me think . . . we haven't gotten to that in school yet. But, but . . ."

"But what?"

"I'm not a little boy anymore."

"I know, I know." Now she was giggling.

"But not such a big boy, either."

"I know, I know."

He leaned down toward her, holding on to two branches.

"How do you know how big I am?"

"Well, I . . ."

"You what?"

"Don't be so nosy, you old fool!"

She was standing beside the apple tree with her head thrown back, her hands on her hips, scolding him.

Albert was hanging six or seven feet above her and he trumpeted, "Girls are stupid!"

"Right, but . . ."

"But they have something we don't have."

She unpinned the brooch from her blouse, the collar fell aside and exposed her breasts.

"I'm going in now for a little rest. A nap at noon is just the thing. It's so reassuring to have an old man up in the tree."

"Sleep tight, old girl! The sight of you from up here, my beauty, is enough for me. I'll watch over your slumbers. But be true to me!"

"I'm going to stretch out on your bed. Maybe I can still smell you from last night."

His voice called down, "Fine, fine. You win! Help me down!"

Once he was safely on solid ground again, he took her in his arms.

"Little Lena, you look down too much! You have to look up once in a while. And what will you see? Me!"

In the afternoon, he practiced "flying." It was a glorious summer day, with the sun blazing overhead. Albert had climbed a ladder on to the roof and with both hands held a large, colorful bath towel above his head.

"There aren't any updrafts! I could easily make it a few yards if I had a good updraft."

"Have you gone completely crazy?" she scolded from down below. "You're not going to make anything! You'll be lucky if you don't break a leg!"

"What do you know about it? A jump from the lowest roof of all time! Come give me a hug, little Lena!"

He ran a few steps as best he could, then bent his knees and jumped. A second later, he was sprawled on the grass and shaking with laughter. Lena ran over to him.

"I wish I hadn't gotten into your bed! It seems to have made you lose your wits. You men! One dumber than the next!"

She tried with all her might to pull him to his feet.

As soon as he was standing, Albert limped around her in circles.

"You have no sense of the higher things. That was a good first try! Just imagine if a storm was sweeping across the bushes and hedges! If it carried me up to the top of the apple tree, I'd be the happiest man in the world! I've dreamed so often of being able to fly—Ikarus! I'll have to build myself some wings, maybe with a steel frame like the pioneers of aviation. This idea—"

He fell forward onto the grass and rolled around holding his ankle and moaning. His whole body was trembling.

"Big talk!" Lena scolded. "And who has to patch you up? Me!"

There was no help for it, his right ankle must be sprained. And although she put salve and bandages on the place where it was bruised and swollen, there woudn't be any dancing tonight. The weary warrior lay stretched out on the narrow sofa with his head in her lap.

"Well, it was worth it anyway! My head in your lap is the best thing I could have wished for!"

"And just now you were singing the praises of flying! Your high opinion of my lap won't last long either."

"The queen beats the jack!"

They listened dreamily to the mysterious Cuban melodies. Albert tried to sing along for a few measures.

"It's not Spanish and it's not Portuguese either. They explained to the girls what the words mean. It's the yearning for home, for those faraway islands that aren't even on most maps. Can you feel the yearning?"

He giggled and Lena ran her hand lightly across his mouth.

Early in the evening, he claimed to be tired out from his adventures. He couldn't wait to be next to her in bed, to embrace her and cover her face with a thousand kisses.

"You're trembling all over," Lena murmured.

"From happiness," he answered.

Later they lay snuggled up together and, wide-awake, he begged her to tell him about herself. "I know so little."

"What do you want to know?"

"Everything! Just start right in anywhere!"

"Hmm. You want a lot from me."

"Please, please?"

"But where should I begin? Okay, since you've shown how smart you are. . . ."

Yes, I'm just a stupid girl. Never had any proper schooling. The nuns who brought me up thought what they gave us was enough. In their opinion, we girls would most likely become nuns ourselves, or bring lots of children into a God-fearing world. And yes, I would have liked to do that. I never would have taken these birth control pills people talk about so much today. They say even little girls, still half children, can't wait to be on them. No, I would have been happy to have lots of children—half a dozen or more, if that's what God wanted. But unfortunately, the miracle of motherhood passed me by. So I got Christie as a present—she was a miracle herself. Like so many people, I got something different than what I wished for.

No one ever asked me where I came from. I was glad of that, for what could I have said? The fact is, I don't come from anywhere. I was an orphan and was put into a Catholic orphanage as a little child. I was too young to remember anything before that. I have no idea where I was born or who my parents were. The priest who prepared us for our first communion told us we were God's children! "You should be proud to be under his special protection!" Fine, I thought, if the priest with his black cassock and serious expression says so. But I still wish I had a father, a mother, and even a sister and a brother. Because unlike God, they'd be flesh and blood. I could touch them. And I understand everything much better when I can touch it. But most important: they'd be there and they'd belong to me. But God—he's far away, invisible, and belongs to everybody. God hovers over us, I can sense him, but I can't touch him.

I loved one of the nuns in our orphanage, really worshipped her: Marie, the youngest nun of all. I think she loved me too. I loved her soft voice that seemed to contain so much understanding and the bright curly hair she would pull out from under her coif to show me. She sometimes gave me an enchanting smile when no one was looking and pressed my hand or gave my back a light, gentle pat. Once she breathed a kiss onto my forehead. I knew then I was saved, but our love had to be kept secret. In the orphanage, all love belonged to God. Later I decided God had sent Marie. I really believed that, and I still do. Someone like me who can perceive God and understand him, someone like that pays attention to his messengers, his celestial emissaries. I pay attention to them; I'm willing and attentive. Marie was one of those emissaries. So was Christie, later on, when I held her in my arms. And then you, Albert, the first time I looked into your eyes.

Once I was mistaken, when I was young and met Jakob, my husband. For this mistake, God punished me severely. Whenever Jakob was anywhere near me, I was beside myself with love—or what I thought was love back then, ignorant as I was. Later, I realized that it wasn't real love but only desire. I was blind. It was a misguided love that led me away from myself and my soul. But that wasn't enough for God.

When I took Jakob as my husband, I made a mistake. The façade of our marriage began to develop cracks right away. He was a good, upstanding Christian, but a strict one, a Christian for whom contrition, vengeance, and penance were more important than love. And he soon lost the face I had constructed for him, the one that had ravished my senses and awakened my desire. He sternly rejected it because he feared any kind of passion. He called it sin even though we were man and wife. Yes, his voice was gentle, but behind it lurked the vehemence of his faith. A faith straight out of the Old Testament, with original sin and the unclean woman. A woman must be chaste, not lustful, and must obey her husband. And so I capitulated. What else could I do? And ended up committing a sin myself when I was unable to mourn his death, but rather rejoiced at my liberation. God had permitted me to begin life anew, my own life!

With Jakob I learned that when a man and a woman lie together without love, it produces no new life, nor that miracle of life, a new human being. So we remained childless, and it overshadowed our marriage more and more as the years went by, stealing even what little happiness we had together. Since Jakob's nightly attempts remained fruitless, he preached abstinence to me. It never would have occurred to him to consult a doctor to find out why we failed to have children. When I suggested that at least I should get an examination, he rejected it outright. No, the hand of man must not be allowed to counteract God's will. So for nights on end, I lay untouched. But he was unable to stick strictly to his grand resolution as planned. From time to time, a frenzy would seize him in the middle of the night. Without the slightest caress or kind word he was suddenly there in the darkness, shoving my legs apart and assaulting me. Even my cries of pain couldn't stop him. He became even more taciturn at home, withdrew more and more into his solitary prayers and only became animated when he set off for choir practice or a choral performance. He never spoke about his work as a teacher. That part of his life remained closed to me from the very first.

I had to weep and plead for a long time before he accepted the idea of adopting a child. At first, he brusquely rejected the possibility: God had come to a different decision, and that was that. Nothing more to be said—those were his exact words. And he remained aloof. Eventually, an anger grew inside me that I had never felt before. I wanted a child! If not from his seed, then a child like I had been—a child of God! He was speechless when I informed him that I had started the process of adopting a daughter. I'd already submitted an application. If he had refused my wish, the first significant wish I ever uttered in many years of married life, I would have turned my back on him forever and gone away. For a few weeks, the only words we spoke to each other were the absolute minimum necessary. Sometimes we didn't speak at all for days on end. But then Christie entered our house, a little package of humanity not yet six months old.

"Here is a child of God," I told my husband, "and her name is Christie."

For just a moment, he smiled. Later I spied him stroking her forehead and cheeks with his fingertips. And when she was baptized, he held her in his arms, but only for a few moments. So he became Christie's father, or as close as that strange man could get to fatherhood.

From that point on, Christie was all my joy and has remained so right up to the present, the second messenger in my life. She illuminated my days just as Marie had. And I could touch her and caress her to my heart's content.

Christie was a good child, intelligent and happy. In fact, she had so much of the wisdom of children that sometimes I had the impression she could already see through the bargain we had struck about her. But if she did, then it was to my benefit. Her brilliant smile, her warm little hands tickling my neck as I carried her through the apartment, were a constantly renewed proof of her love and of her gratitude.

Our relationship changed when Gloria entered her life. Christie was already a big girl and always a step ahead of me in intelligence. Later she outpaced me by many more steps, but despite that undeniable distance, it never separated us. Christie turned more and more to Gloria's family, but it was never clear if the impulse was hers or if Gloria had her under a spell. When you saw the two of them walking arm in arm, one glance was enough to tell that they belonged together—sisters in spirit, but also in flesh and blood, two tall, graceful angels, two messengers from heaven whose long, blond, windblown hair would make your heart stand still. They seemed made for each other.

Then I met you—Gloria's father—even though we only saw each other for a few brief minutes. You were standing pensively at our front door, looking down with an almost imperceptible smile on you face. You were handsome, but it was your eyes that particularly struck me: a look that seemed to come from far away, a look that saw everything without passing judgment on it. A forgiving look. You stood there, a little awkward, but quietly, as if we had known each other for a long time. You were Gloria's father but I knew that in her dreams, Christie had long since made you into her father too. It was clear why. But I was touched by the way you were with Gloria. And I knew more than you thought. You spread your arms a little, not demanding, but as if to say—I'll hold you in my arms, but only if you want me to. You loved her. My woman's intuition told me how much love you were capable of.

. . .

Without knowing it, Christie had brought us together. We only exchanged a few words, insignificant ones, no doubt. Just before you left down the dark hall of our apartment—you and Gloria, leaning her head against your shoulder—you rested your hands with their slender, long fingers for just a moment on my shoulders. And I could sense how much the darkness was already tugging at Gloria like an evil spirit.

It was no surprise that I couldn't help loving you. From the very first moment. An unattainable love, of course. There was no doubt about that, but it didn't bother me. I had already made my decision: an unattainable love was better than a love that is picked apart piece by piece until nothing's left but emptiness and loneliness. Believe me, Albert, you were my third messenger!

Lena paused, the silence next to her is almost palpable. My God, she thought, I've talked more at one stretch than ever before in my life and he's fallen asleep. He'll never know he is my love.

With powerful strokes, Albert swims deeper and deeper. He's amazed at how well he's managing in the depths of the ocean. In the distance he can see the two girls, still half children, swimming with brisk, rapid movements that remind him of fish. They're naked, the way he saw them that time in the mountain lake: slim bodies with little dark patches in their armpits and below their bellies. He catches up to them, close enough to touch. But they obviously don't see him. They're preoccupied with themselves. They hold hands and smile at each other. Suddenly they disappear from view. He catches just a momentary glimpse of their bright bodies far below him, getting smaller and smaller in the darkness of the night.

The water grows darker. Just above him he sees powerful wings with tremendous reach, beating slowly like some unimaginable fairy-tale creature. Why can't he remember? He's sure he knows the name of this monster, proceeding on its deliberate way, every inch of it disdaining to notice him. Who is this majestic being?

Then, suddenly, the girls are beside him again, their skin sparkling like fish scales in the pulsing shafts of sunlight. They come up close to him and their faces look like they're laughing at him. Gloria points her finger at him. Only now he becomes aware of her body. Her large breasts brush against him. He's never seen her like this! Or has he? When was it? But then there's another woman facing him—is she upright or floating? Is she standing on a rock? It's not Ann and it's not Lena. No, he doesn't know this woman. Strange, she's wearing a dark dress that billows out sideways. He's surprised at her small, bare feet. They look like a child's feet. Is it Ann after all? No, it's Lena! Or someone else?

It's high time he returned to the surface. He's running out of air. With a shout of relief Albert bursts from the water and finds himself trembling in Lena's arms. She strokes his forehead reassuringly.

He murmurs, "It was a manta! A manta! . . . I saw it!"

Ann's letter was lying on the breakfast table. Albert didn't ask how it got there. He calmly sipped his tea and finished his bread and honey. Then he slit open the envelope, took out the letter, smoothed it out on the table, and put on his glasses. Lena sat across from him. He read aloud, with a clear, firm voice; there can't be any secrets between them.

> *Dear Albert,*
>
> *I was wrong. I did you an injustice. Everything started out so well. With Father's approval, I was head over heels in love with you. But that began to fade when I felt closed in by our cramped quarters. Then, instead of having any understanding for you, I started looking for my young woman's image of what the man of my dreams should be. And in the process I started to neglect you. Not your body, but your heart (which is much more important) and finally your soul. Have I lost you? And why didn't you stop me, confront me, put me in my place? I can't help thinking it was a little your fault, too.*
>
> *Sometimes a woman needs to be told what's what. You were too gentle, too understanding, I'm sorry to say. You should have taken hold of me and given me a good shaking. Maybe that would have helped.*
>
> *As Mary lay dying in my arms, I looked into her fading eyes and realized how short life is, how mortal we are. I also saw our poor, beloved Gloria in her eyes and knew I had been unjust to her because of my unspeakable pride. In the last days before Mary's death, she and I talked a lot about the father who dominated our lives so much. She freed herself from him early on but paid a heavy price for it. And we two sisters became enemies. In my eyes, she was always the traitor, the bad sister, and I was the good and grateful child. Now we had made our peace and with whatever strength she had left, she helped me free myself from my father. It was much too long coming, I know. What a terrible thing it was! The detours I had to*

make! You showed me understanding and I failed to show any for you.

Yes, I've made my peace, not just with her but also with Gloria and with you. I ask you to forgive me. But if you want your freedom from me, my darling, just say the word. I must not be any more burden to you on the short road we still have to travel.

One word about Anton, our son. I saw the way he was in your shadow from the time he was a little boy and I resented it. You're such a principled man you never wanted to acknowledge that shadow. But the shadow a father casts on his maturing son can be the darkest one of all. You loved Gloria with all your heart—there was no room for anyone else. And so I took his side and resolved to protect him.

How short life is! Will you share the little time left with me? I'm asking you to.

Your Ann
(of long ago, and of tomorrow, if you want her).

Albert's voice died away. He was not even aware he had read the letter out loud, clearly, word for word. The old man looked over at Lena until she finally dropped her eyes. She sat huddled in her chair, unmoving. She knew: he's going to leave me! I felt it. He'll go back to her!

He stayed another day, said nothing. Early in the evening, they walked into the woods, hardly exchanging a word. But he took her hand often and with a beating heart, she felt how his hand trembled. He needs me, she thought, how he needs me! She wanted to say something, but the words stuck in her throat.

They felt so choked off and the pain was so real that she put her left hand up to her neck.

Far down in the darkening valley they saw deer for the first time. The buck was grazing near a thicket and looked back repeatedly. Albert and Lena didn't dare to emerge from the trees. They held their breath and moved more and more slowly. Then they stopped completely. Just in front of them there was a fawn. It looked at them and they could see deep into its eyes. Then it scampered off. The deer continued to graze. Suddenly the buck swung his head around, let out a short bellow, and in a split second the herd disappeared into the underbrush as if they'd never been there.

Albert and Lena climbed up to the hunter's stand near where the buck had been, sat huddled together on the narrow platform, leaning forward and intently scanning the clearing below. But the deer had been warned off and didn't return.

Evening had fallen in the valley. It got cool. It was time to go back. With melancholy hearts they climbed back down the wooden ladder. Albert descended cautiously. He gave the stand a long, backward look. Will he ever sit up there again, as happy as he was today? Then he followed Lena back through the dark forest. She knew every step of the way; he wouldn't get lost with her in the lead.

He lagged behind. She didn't turn around to look for him but continued resolutely forward on her short, strong legs. When he caught up, he was out of breath.

"It's too bad you know the way so well. I would love to—"

"Oh, you men! A little detour here, a little detour there, the goal can always wait!"

"You know better—"

"You know just as well as I do, don't pretend you don't! It's just time . . . if you could just have more time, time for a little more fun, for this and that."

Her voice was almost cracking. He had never seen her like this. He was silent, abashed. When they reached the giant anthill at the edge of the woods, Albert stopped and stood for a long time contemplating the tall, mysterious structure that housed all those thousands upon thousands of lives.

One fierce kick would destroy it, expose its secrets. He paused there for a long time, thinking. Although night had fallen, Lena had gone on ahead. Finally he groped his way the last few yards out of the woods and emerged into the pale light bathing the hilltop. He was moving his lips, talking to himself, arguing with himself. He got excited, slapped his cheek with his open palm, bit his lip so hard to control his rising anger that it hurt and a little warm blood trickled down his chin.

Down at the house, the lights were shining through the darkness. Lena got back quite a while ago. The sight calmed him and he trotted wearily down the sloping meadow to the house.

That night they went to bed in their separate rooms but left the doors wide open. Before falling asleep, she heard his familiar voice.

"Good night, beloved Lena! Sleep well!"

His voice was bright and clear. Didn't he say "beloved Lena"? Yes, she had heard it clearly, no doubt about it. In a few moments sleep embraced her.

He lay awake in the middle of the night. It was the hour when anxiety and fear had attacked him so often in the past. He heard her regular breathing. Can there be any greater happiness, he wondered. Just one more breath, then he couldn't stay in bed any longer and stumbled the few steps over to her through the darkness. Not until he got in next to her and put out his hand to touch her did he notice how much his arms were trembling. He whispered to her, "It's just my joy!"

Lena pulled him closer.

"You're cold, but I have enough warmth to spare."

He gave a quiet laugh. "You're a seductress! That's a crime when you're young, but what about when you're old? What then?"

"It's a mitigating circumstance if you're in love."

They lay together without speaking for a long time. His arms had stopped shaking.

"Won't you finish telling me your story? I love listening to you, Lena."

Now it was her turn to laugh.

"So you can fall asleep again? No, not again! I told you everything, my darling. But what about you? I think you've still got something you'd like to get off your chest."

"Then you know more than I do. . . . But maybe you're right. Why do you always have to be right? Yes, there is something . . ."

"Good. I'm listening. . . ."

"No, it's too embarrassing."

"Of course it is. And don't you think I was embarrassed before I got in bed with you?"

"I wasn't!"

"But you said there was 'something' . . . ?"

Albert pushed himself up to a sitting position:

. . .

I've suppressed it for a long time. And it was a long time ago. Once in the middle of the night I woke up and tiptoed to the bathroom I shared with Ann. On the way back to the room that had just recently been set up for me so I wouldn't disturb Ann in the night, I saw a ray of light in the stairwell from the third floor. Was our child Gloria unable to sleep? Had something happened? On my way upstairs, careful not to let the floorboards creak too loudly underfoot, I thought, she's not a child any longer. She's a big girl.

I followed the light. The door to her bathroom was open a crack. Cautiously, I peered inside, worried I would startle her in the middle of the night when she thought she was alone. In fact, there was no child in the shower. No, the low light fell from behind onto the body of a woman: strange, beautiful, sensuous. She turned slowly toward me, her eyes closed, her wet hair hanging over her face in strands down to her shoulders. The glass shower stall that separated us was steamed up. But I saw enough, saw the young woman over whose body the water ran, rinsing off the soapy foam. I caught my breath: this woman with full breasts, hips, the brush of pubic hair below the pale dome of her belly, the rounded thighs—was that my daughter? Was it really her, this woman I'd never seen before, hadn't even guessed the existence of, who in the blink of an eye transformed me, as I stood there, from a loving, caring father into a hungry, greedy wolf? No, no, that wasn't my child Gloria! It was a nocturnal delusion, witchcraft, an evil seduction that had befallen my unsuspecting, innocent self.

She shut the water off. Individual drops still ran down her body. With her hand she brushed them off her skin, her breasts, and her white thighs. Her hand rested a few seconds on her belly, her fingers splayed over the dark pubic hair. Then she stepped out of the stall onto the mat, picked up a bath towel hanging from the towel bar, spread it out across her shoulders as she turned toward the mirror, and wrapped it around her hair with a practiced motion. Now I was looking at her long, slim back. I saw the sharp inward curve of her spine as it descended in a long line from her shoulder blades to the cleft far below. My heart stood still, I had almost stopped breathing. My senses were in an unimagined uproar, had taken possession of me unawares. I was almost crazy. Was this me, this man standing here at the door staring into the bathroom in his rumpled pajamas and tousled hair? Was I really the man I had thought I was up until then? Who was I, anyway? The person I had always thought I was, someone incapable of being overcome by his impulses as I was now? Whence this panting wolf who had entered my body and was stalking his prey? Gloria had dried herself off from top to toe and wrapped herself in the towel.

She looked into the mirror hanging above the sink. The steam was clearing, and her gaze met mine. We looked into each other's eyes without moving, without speaking. I was paralyzed. Had she known I was there? How long had I been standing there watching her? How much time had passed? Her expression was deeply serious as her face gradually regained its familiarity. Finally, she found a way to break the spell.

"Come on in!"

Her voice sounded very far away. She gestured to a stool in the corner and I obediently sat down on it, my eyes on the floor, looking at her feet. How small and innocent they looked. What else could I do? If I mumbled one or two words—perhaps it was a question, maybe not—they were garbled and meaningless.

She said, "You look tired! You should be in bed."

In fact, now that she said it, I was seized by a weariness that made me almost unconscious. This woman, my daughter, seemed to possess magical power over me. Almost as naturally as during the day, she continued to speak while running a comb through her long hair.

"You're wondering why I'm taking a shower in the middle of the night. I felt so dirty. I often do since I've become a woman."

She again urged me to go back to bed. I pulled myself together, somehow got to my feet, and crept downstairs as I had come, once again a broken old man now seized by profound sadness.

I looked back up the stairs and saw her, still clad in the bath towel, waving good night to me.

"Don't worry, Father! Be happy."

I lay awake for a long time, immobile on my bed that was suddenly so narrow. There were tears in my eyes. How could I not worry? How could I be happy when I had desired that woman with a vehemence I had never known before? I was a beast released from captivity, desiring my own daughter. Images and thoughts flickered through my head like lightning. Guilt! How could I ever expiate my guilt? How could I ever again be the carefree person Gloria had told me to be? Don't worry, Father! Was I to blame for my daughter's fate? Was it my fault?

Albert heaved a sigh. He waited for her to respond, but she said nothing. Why doesn't she say something? he thought.

"Why don't you say something?"

Lena took her time. She seemed to be thinking. Finally, she said, "There's not much to say. Didn't Gloria herself tell you not to worry? Isn't that enough? Go to sleep now! Let your memories rest in peace!"

On the following morning, everything had changed. Both of them could feel time reaching into their lives again. They'd had so much to tell each other in the past few days, but now they breakfasted in silence. No, there was nothing left to say. Their love was yesterday. Today, their tumultuous feelings had grown still. As if their pleasantries and attentiveness to each other were forgotten. They eyed each other like strangers. It was especially Lena who was on her guard. What would he do? She watched every move he made. When he finally got up slowly from the table, her eyes followed him doubtfully. He left the kitchen without a word. Lena heard the front door open and close again. She stayed sitting at the kitchen table as if under a spell. She could see him out in the garden, walking slowly up and down the lawn. He seemed to be feeling fine without her. Was he puffing out his cheeks the way he did when he breathed in the fresh air? It gave him a new lease on life, he once said. What was he thinking now? Did he have a plan?

Lena was tired. As so often in the past, she felt like she was no use to anyone. What a difference, what a letdown compared to the previous days and nights! She heard his steps in his bedroom. He must have come back in. That was how he walked when he was tired—dragging his feet a bit. She stood up quietly, and tiptoed over to his room, wearing the slippers she'd gotten out for the first time since he'd been in the house. Aha, she thought when she saw him taking his underwear out of the wardrobe and piling it on the unmade bed. No wonder his hands were trembling again. Now she knew. She stepped into the room, pushed Albert gently aside, already had his suitcase in her other hand.

Suddenly he froze, standing next to her. His head wobbled quickly from side to side.

"What's wrong?"

Lena tried to support him.

"I can't . . . I feel paralyzed."

She pulled over a stool and helped him sit down.

"Take a rest! There's no hurry."

After a while, he nodded to her.

"I'm feeling better now."

She reached for the suitcase.

"You want me to?"

He nodded again.

There was not much to pack. He was only intending to stay for a few days. Just while Christie was still here, before she had to go back. Yes, it turned out to be longer, thought Lena, and they were overwhelmingly beautiful days.

Once the bag was packed and standing in the hallway, Lena helped Albert into the living room once more, gave him a cup of coffee, and gazed at him for a long time.

"So now what? Why don't you let her go? Let her die. Can you finally allow her to die, now that she's been dead so long?"

They sat close together.

"How long?" said Albert.

"Well, more than two years have passed, after all. Two summers. The leaves have died twice, the earth has frozen, and then spring has come with new buds—all that once and then once more. That's a long time, isn't it?"

"Yes, you're right. It's a damn long time. . . ."

"Well, Albert?"

"It's so hard for me. You don't understand. If I let her go now, just set her free out of fear, then I'll be left alone. Alone with all my fears, all alone with my fear. That's hard. It's too much to ask."

"What kind of fear is it? Fear of life? Fear of death?"

"If I knew that, I'd be cured. No, it's neither, it's more than that. Just plain fear. Maybe because I'm here. It's so hard to find words for it—the incomprehensible, nothingness . . . the abyss . . . they're all just words! I've been hiding from it. With my love for her. My love grew more and more, became boundless, unlimited. I thought I was saved. When she suddenly was gone, my grief was all I had left. And now I should give that up too? How should I go about it? Am I able to?"

"Maybe the loss of the love that has died weighs just as much as the fear of being alone."

"Perhaps. I've got to face up to it. I don't think I have a choice any longer. Not now."

There were tears in his eyes. He stammered, "Think of me! Don't forget me! And don't be sad if I—"

She interrupted him.

"If you leave now. But I will be sad. I'm already sad. You've got to let me be sad. But what does sadness weigh against my happiness? It was more than I could have hoped for. Believe me, I'm a lucky woman!"

Timidly, he reached for her hands. At last, he heard his own voice, wooden and strange. "I think I'd better take the train. I'll take a chance on traveling by myself. It's not too far. Please call a taxi to take me to the station. I can make the noon train."

She nodded. "Look outside! The taxi's already here, in front of the house. He's been waiting a good long time already. But he's not going to take you to the station. He's going to take you straight home."

He raised his hands, which had begun to shake, and his legs were also rhythmically trembling. Lena laid her hand on his knee.

"Don't be angry with me. I had no other choice. I could lead you through the woods, but not when a train whisks you away to unknown places and you disappear. Don't forget: I need you. I need to know that you're there somewhere. And happy!"

She helped him up. His legs were still unsteady.

"Thank you, thank you . . ."

Lena took his arm as they walked slowly out the front door.

"Look, your bag is already in the cab. Can you hear the motor running?"

Albert pulled her to him.

"I can hear your heart beating."

"Don't forget: try not to worry, try to be happy!"

He bent down to her, closed his eyes and kissed her gently on the lips. He put his hand on her shoulder and gave it a little squeeze. His hand was steady. When he reached the garden gate, he turned around once more. He saw her pale face framed by the green plants. She broke into a wide smile that dissolved into a thousand tiny lines.